Dramatic Debuts
Volume 2

If I Were Your Superhero by Laignee Barron

A Funeral for Mittens by Samuel French

Making Babies by Paxton Grey Farrar

Baker's Plays
7611 Sunset Blvd.
Los Angeles, CA 90042
bakersplays.com

I0741890

MUSIC USE NOTE

Licensees are solely responsible for obtaining formal written permission from copyright owners to use copyrighted music in the performance of this play and are strongly cautioned to do so. If no such permission is obtained by the licensee, then the licensee must use only original music that the licensee owns and controls. Licensees are solely responsible and liable for all music clearances and shall indemnify the copyright owners of the play and their licensing agent, Baker's Plays, against any costs, expenses, losses and liabilities arising from the use of music by licensees.

THE BAKER'S PLAYS HIGH SCHOOL PLAYWRITING COMPETITION

Baker's Plays has been an advocate for theater in schools for over one hundred years. In the spirit of that commitment, we offer the Baker's High School Playwriting Competition for all High School-aged dramatists interested in the craft of playwriting. It is our hope that this competition will encourage aspiring High School authors to explore the creative possibilities of writing for the stage.

This volume of *Dramatic Debuts* represents the culmination of the 2009 competition. The three plays included in this book display what we at Baker's Plays felt was the strongest understanding of writing for the stage. The plays included in this volume are:

First place

If I Were your Superhero by Laignee Barron

Second place

A Funeral for Mittens by Samuel French

Third place

Making Babies by Paxton Grey Farrar

We congratulate these three writers and thank all who participated in the 2009 competition.

For information as to how enter the Baker's Plays High School Playwriting Competition as well as information on past competition winners, visit our website at **bakersplays.com**.

CONTENTS

IF I WERE YOUR SUPERHERO

by Laignee Barron

CHARACTERS

Kylie
Mother
Girl
Manager
Gunther
Jed
Grandma
Mrs. Hunter

ABOUT THE PLAYWRIGHT

In addition to playwriting, Laignee Barron loves the *San Francisco Chronicle*, staircases, 3 am adventures, black and white movies, coffee, the Oxford comma, and bookstores with long hours. Laignee also writes poetry and prose, and was introduced to playwriting at the Ojai Playwrights Conference. A 2008 Scholastic Art and Writing Awards winner for journalism and fiction, Laignee's work has won the California Young Playwrights Contest, the 2009 Young Playwrights, Inc. National Competition, the Rubicon Playwrights Festival, and has been featured at Theater 150. Currently a freshman at Wesleyan University, Laignee plans to continue writing as long as pen and paper will continue to indulge her. Laignee is grateful to Baker's Plays and its sponsors for a wonderful opportunity, and thanks her wonderful drama teachers and her infinitely supportive family and friends.

Scene One

*(**KYLIE** is in her room listening to the radio and getting ready for a play. She is sitting at her desk in front of her mirror. On the desk is a stuffed octopus and a clutter of books. **KYLIE** is wearing a costume of sorts, has glitter on her face and is brushing her obviously already well-brushed hair. She stops, puts down the brush, and puts on lipstick. She then stands, looks in the mirror and puts on a pair of fairy wings.)*

KYLIE. Mom! Dress rehearsal starts in 10 minutes.

(no response)

MOM!

*(**KYLIE** walks out of her room to the other side of the stage, which becomes dimly lit. It's a living room where Kylie's **MOTHER** is lying asleep on the sofa. Beer bottles adorn the coffee table but **KYLIE** doesn't appear to notice or care. **KYLIE** turns on a lamp – the light wakes her **MOTHER** up.)*

Mom?

MOTHER. Kylie…? What –

KYLIE. I thought you said you were going to take me to rehearsal.

MOTHER. What's going on?

KYLIE. My dress rehearsal. Without me.

MOTHER. Huh?

KYLIE. C'mon, *Midsummer Night's Dream.* I'm Titania, the Fairy Queen. You knew about this.

MOTHER. Oh God, Kylie I'm too tired.

KYLIE. You promised you would take me.

MOTHER. I've got a horrible headache.

KYLIE. You're drunk. Great.

MOTHER. Isn't there some one else who can drive you?

KYLIE. No.

MOTHER. The bus?

KYLIE. Stopped running an hour ago.

MOTHER. Your director?

KYLIE. The phone's out again.

MOTHER. What?

KYLIE. You didn't pay the bills.

MOTHER. Oh God.

KYLIE. This is the last run-thru before the show.

MOTHER. Where'd you put the bill?

KYLIE. Do you know how hard I worked to get this role?

MOTHER. How long has the phone been off for?

KYLIE. I've been memorizing lines and rehearsing for three months.

MOTHER. Do you still have the letter?

KYLIE. MOM! Goddamnit!

MOTHER. Can't you skip tonight?

KYLIE. No. I told you Mrs. A. warned me that if I missed this show or was late again she'd give the role to the understudy.

MOTHER. You never told me that.

KYLIE. YES, I did!!

MOTHER. They changed my shift at work. I have to get up in four hours.

KYLIE. Bullshit.

MOTHER. Get Jed to take you.

KYLIE. Jed's not here.

MOTHER. What are you talking about?

KYLIE. Christ, you're not even here when you're here.

MOTHER. Don't talk to me like that!

    (pause)

    Ok, you know what, just go get my keys. I'll take you.

KYLIE. You're drunk!

(**KYLIE** *moves towards the door.*)

MOTHER. Where are you going?

KYLIE. I'm walking to my rehearsal.

MOTHER. No, you're not.

(**KYLIE** *goes back to her room, slamming the door. She takes off the wings, throws them. She curls into a fetal position on the floor.*)

I don't know what you want me to say, Kylie, or what you want me to do. You can't just demand to be somewhere, when you need to be there. I have other responsibilities. I have a job to think about. Maybe you should consider priorities. I try, goddamnit, Kylie. I try so hard for you…

(*She breaks down.*)

It wasn't my fault. I tried, Kylie. I try.

(**KYLIE** *takes out textbooks and notebooks from her back pack. She picks one up, it has "FREAK" markered on the front.* **KYLIE** *flings it across the room, grabs a stuffed octopus from her desk and sits on her bed hugging it to her chest just as her* **MOTHER** *takes a pillow, sitting on the sofa and hugs it to her own chest.*)

Scene Two

(**KYLIE** *is working at the grocery store. She is standing at the cash register doing absolutely nothing, and looking thoroughly bored. A little* **GIRL** *about ten or twelve years old walks up and puts a pack of gum on the counter.* **KYLIE** *glares at her.*)

GIRL. Hello!!

KYLIE. What?!

GIRL. I want to buy this gum.

KYLIE. Wonderful.

(There is a pause and then **KYLIE** *points towards a door)*

The exit's that way.

GIRL. What about the gum?

KYLIE. What about it?

GIRL. I want to buy it.

KYLIE. Intriguing. I have a break in a few minutes, why don't you tell me more then.

GIRL. Can I buy the gum?

KYLIE. No.

GIRL. Why not?

KYLIE. Because that happens to be the flavor of gum you aren't allowed to buy.

GIRL. Who says?

KYLIE. Me.

GIRL. But, this is the flavor of gum I chew.

(She opens her mouth to reveal a wad of pink gum to demonstrate.)

And I need more.

KYLIE. Really? 'Cuz that's the type of gum all evil, unjust people happen to chew. Therefore, I must stop you.

GIRL. You're really weird.

KYLIE. So I've been told.

(The **GIRL** *turns around to where the gum is stacked and pulls a different pack of gum from another box. She puts the one she wanted to buy back and places the new one on the counter top.)*

GIRL. Can I buy this one?

KYLIE. *(considers for the moment)* Nope.

GIRL. Why not?!

KYLIE. Bad after taste.

GIRL. You act like you're God or something.

(The **GIRL** *turns and puts the gum back. She then takes a pack of gum from every box except the ones she's already tried. She dumps them all on the counter.)*

Can I buy any of these?

(**KYLIE** *digs through the pile and picks a cotton candy flavored Bubble Yum pack. She shoves the rest further down the register.* **KYLIE** *scans the gums through the register. She repeats the process six times while humming. The* **GIRL** *is impatiently watching* **KYLIE** *and fiddling with her hair.* **KYLIE** *pretends not to notice.*)

Could you hurry?

KYLIE. Don't feel like it.

GIRL. Please?!!

KYLIE. *(rolls her eyes and punches something into the keyboard and stops scanning the gum)* Right then. $6.50 please.

GIRL. What?! That's not fair. It says $1!

KYLIE. Unfortunately we don't offer lay away.

GIRL. Do you have a boss?

KYLIE. Yeah.

GIRL. Where?

KYLIE. *(shrugs)* Feel free to look.

GIRL. Could you *please* get him?

(**MANAGER** *enters.*)

MANAGER. What's the problem here?

(**KYLIE** *and the* **GIRL** *both start talking at once, but the* **MANAGER** *turns to* **KYLIE** *and tells her to be quiet.*)

MANAGER. *(to the girl)* Yes, miss?

GIRL. I was just trying to buy a pack of gum. But she wouldn't let me until finally she chooses one and is making me pay $6.50 but I only have $3!

MANAGER. You can take your gum compliments of the store. I can guarantee this will never happen again. My apologies.

(*The* **GIRL** *exits with the gum. The manager turns to speak with* **KYLIE**.)

MANAGER. Kindly explain.

KYLIE. You wouldn't understand.

MANAGER. It's my job to understand. Yours is to process the sale, hand the customer their receipt and tell them, "Have a nice day," it isn't too difficult is it?

KYLIE. No, and I did that. I just added a few steps in between.

MANAGER. Oh really? $6.50?

KYLIE. The world is just poised at 6.5 right now. It's six and a half minutes until my break. I got up at 6:50 this morning and I work a 6 and a 1/2 hour shift. 6.5 is the number of miles from here to my house, and 6.5 thousand miles is how far away I'd like to be. You've made me furious enough to want to rip up my paycheck 6 and a 1/2 times, but that would've been 6 and a 1/2 times that I wasted money I've been saving for a plane ticket to go to Boston to live with my brother. I've been working here for 6 and a half weeks and judging by that look on your face I'll probably be working here for only another 6 and a half minutes.

(**KYLIE** *takes her apron off. She starts to walk away.*)

MANAGER. Kylie?

KYLIE. Yeah…

(**MANAGER** *stares for a moment and then shakes his head.*)

KYLIE. What?

MANAGER. What do you think you deserve after that stunt with the little girl?

KYLIE. I dunno. You'll probably invent something utterly debasing and humiliating in attempts to expose that underneath the rotten layers of my soul there lies a conscience.

MANAGER. How about 6 and a 1/2 weeks in customer service in the returns and complaints department?

KYLIE. How about not?

MANAGER. You could use the training.

KYLIE. Then how about going through regular training again?

MANAGER. No. Unless you really want to be fired this time that's your option. Last chance.

KYLIE. Fine, fire me.

MANAGER. Is that a threat Kylie, because I'm trying to do you a favor.

KYLIE. No, that's me bored with punch cards and suffering the iron fist of corporate America.

MANAGER. *(sighing)* Go take your ten-minute break and then we'll talk.

KYLIE. No thanks. I don't want to mess with or destroy my stupidly, perfectly, mathematically balanced world.

(**KYLIE** *starts walking out again.*)

Scene Three

(**KYLIE** *is sitting on the sidewalk in front of her house looking miserable and wearing the wings from her play. She takes a shoebox out of her bag, opens the box and lifts out a few of the objects and looks at them.* **GUNTHER** *walks up with his backpack slung on one shoulder looking equally miserable.* **GUNTHER** *sits down next to* **KYLIE.**)

GUNTHER. Hi.

KYLIE. Um…hi.

GUNTHER. *(referring to the box)* What's that?

KYLIE. Nothing.

(*She quickly puts the box back in her bag.*)

GUNTHER. Oh. Life sucks, doesn't it?

KYLIE. Sorry?!

GUNTHER. Don't be sorry, it's not your fault.

KYLIE. That's not what I meant.

GUNTHER. Then why'd you say it?

KYLIE. It's what I meant to say, it's just –

GUNTHER. I thought it wasn't what you wanted to say.

KYLIE. I wanted to say it –

GUNTHER. But you didn't want to mean it?

KYLIE. NO!!!!!!!!

GUNTHER. You're very frustrated.

KYLIE. Yeah, whatever.

GUNTHER. I'm sorry.

KYLIE. *(taking a deep breath)* That's just it! I didn't mean I was sorry, like apologetic. I meant what you said was unclear to me.

GUNTHER. Oh. Then why didn't you say that?

KYLIE. I did!

GUNTHER. No, you apologized. You're supposed to say, "excuse me," or, "could you explain," or, "I'm not sure I understood."

KYLIE. Oh my God.

GUNTHER. I think you should come to my school. *(nods head as if to affirm that his decision is a good one)* My teacher's very good at explaining things like that. She says that self-expression is our tool to understanding each other.

KYLIE. Deep.

GUNTHER. What's deep?

KYLIE. What your teacher told you.

GUNTHER. Huh?

KYLIE. *(sighing)* Never mind.

    (pause)

KYLIE. Who are you anyway?

GUNTHER. My name's, Gut, Gunth, Gunt, Gehtr, Gu, Greth, GUNTHER!

KYLIE. Uh sure.

GUNTHER. No, it's Guth, Gut, Gunt –

KYLIE. Don't hurt yourself Gunther.

GUNTHER. My name's not Gunther!!!

KYLIE. Then why'd you say it?

GUNTHER. I didn't mean to! You must have made me.

KYLIE. I didn't make you do anything.

GUNTHER. For your information I'm named after some folk singer person. And you're annoying.

KYLIE. You're much more annoying!

GUNTHER. Fine.

KYLIE. Fine!

GUNTHER. Don't copy me.

KYLIE. I wasn't trying to!

GUNTHER. But you did.

KYLIE. Yeah, so? What do you care?

GUNTHER. You're mean.

KYLIE. Not generally.

GUNTHER. *(sighs)* I told you, life sucks.

KYLIE. *(laughs)*

GUNTHER. Don't laugh at me.

KYLIE. I've never heard or seen an eight year-old say that "Life Sucks" before.

GUNTHER. I'm ten, thank you.

KYLIE. Excuuussee me.

GUNTHER. You're one of those tall people who picks on everyone else just because they're littler, aren't you.

KYLIE. No, not generally.

GUNTHER. You mean you're a gentle giant?

KYLIE. Um, no.

GUNTHER. Well then, you must be a pirate.

KYLIE. I've only ever illegally downloaded what I as an American teenager am entitled to, thanks.

GUNTHER. Maybe some sort of fairy with dilapidated wings?

KYLIE. Most people call me Kylie, but sure, whatever you say.

GUNTHER. Cool! I found my power, the ability to tell other heroes their powers.

(**KYLIE** *rolls finger by the side of her head, indicating that she thinks that* **GUNTHER** *is insane.*)

GUNTHER. Why are you wearing wings anyways?

KYLIE. They were for a play I was supposed to be the lead in.

GUNTHER. Oh. What does Kyrie mean?

KYLIE. Huh?

GUNTHER. Your name, Kyrie.

KYLIE. It's Kylie, and I don't know that it means anything.

GUNTHER. I like Kyrie better. That's what I'll call you.

KYLIE. Good for you.

GUNTHER. What's your favorite book? Mine's *Red Fish, Blue Fish.*

KYLIE. One fish, two fish?

GUNTHER. You've read it?

KYLIE. A long time ago. Look, um, Gunther –

GUNTHER. That's not my name!! It's Gu –

KYLIE. *(hastily cuts* **GUNTHER** *short)* Ok, fine. Whatever your name is, I'm sure that you have things you want to be doing other than hanging around with people like me, and I should probably go and –

GUNTHER. Nope. I don't have annnyywhere or annnyyy-place I need to be. I told you, life sucks, so people like you are ok with me.

KYLIE. Honored.

(*pause*)

KYLIE. Why do you keep saying that?

GUNTHER. What?

KYLIE. Your, "Life Sucks" quote.

GUNTHER. Well, you see, when you're littler, nobody listens to you. You're just a stupid baby. No one pays atten-tion, except when you've done something wrong. So I told them I didn't want to play the stupid basket-ball game, I'm not good at it. But they said I had to. Nobody understands.

KYLIE. Don't expect it to get better as you get older.

GUNTHER. I don't. *(after a pause)* What's your problem?

KYLIE. What?!

GUNTHER. Well, what have you been doing sitting on the side of the road looking depressed?

KYLIE. Maybe I just wanted to sit here.

GUNTHER. Everyone's got problems.

KYLIE. What are you, a mini-shrink?

GUNTHER. That's off the topic!

KYLIE. What topic?!

GUNTHER. Your problems!

KYLIE. I don't have any.

GUNTHER. Liar.

KYLIE. You're a strange little kid! Don't you want to go play with your friends, run around? Feel free, to um… leave. I'll just enjoy my patch of sidewalk alone.

GUNTHER. Why is this your sidewalk?

KYLIE. *(points behind her)* Because that happens to be my house.

GUNTHER. It's really ugly!

KYLIE. Thank you. You don't have to look at it, you know.

GUNTHER. Sor-ry! *(He moves over to the next concrete slat.)* Is that better?

KYLIE. No!

GUNTHER. You know that that sidewalk belongs to the city and not to you?

KYLIE. *(gets up)* Fine! Take it. Move right in, why don't you! Why don't you take the house too, since it charmed you so much?! I only wanted a small space to sit and be alone, but fine, have it. Why would I care about any-thing?

GUNTHER. I'm sorry, Kyrie.

KYLIE. *(sighs)* Yeah.

GUNTHER. I'll leave if you want me to.

KYLIE. I was just…just upset.

GUNTHER. *(moves closer to her)* What's wrong?

KYLIE. I…nothing.

GUNTHER. What?

KYLIE. I'm just tired.

GUNTHER. And?

KYLIE. It's just that I'm tired of everyone judging me. I'm sick of people who screw up as often as I do telling me I'm wrong. What I wear, how I talk, what I do, or what I don't do. I'm not the one to blame, for my mother, for my father, for my brother. I want to come home and not be locked out, I want my mom to be happy, I want my brother to come back, I want someone to care. And I want my mom to just…notice I exist, for her to show that she thinks about me every once in a great while, and to figure out what's important to me, or where I need to be or how I'm going to get there. You know some of the stuff she pulls is just funny. When I was eight she left me at the dentist's. I sat in that chair, just sat and sat with the little bib on and the dentist's tools out in front of me, so proud I had no cavities. But I had no one to share the revelation with, I was there for four hours calling my home phone from the receptionist's office every ten minutes. When the dentist's assistants started wondering if they should call the police to take me home, I left, too embarrassed to say anything. I walked the 22 blocks back to my house. I was eight. So you know, maybe just for once I'd like if someone looked out for me. I'm so tired of waiting for things to get better, but whatever I do I can't ever make them better. I feel like I always have to be the strong one, the one looking out for everyone else. But for right now, I just don't want to hurt anymore.

(She pauses and then sighs.) I'm sorry. I'm sure that's more than you asked to hear.

GUNTHER. That's ok. I kind of understood, at least the part about no one understanding. *(pause)* You know what I do when I feel bad?

KYLIE. No, what?

(*GUNTHER puts down his backpack on the sidewalk, opens it, and then digs through it. He pulls out several colorful magazines and comics then drops them on the sidewalk. He lifts one up and shows KYLIE.*)

GUNTHER. I read Aquaman comics. *(He shrugs.)* Want to see one? *(handing her a comic)* They're really Miss Nanny's. She had them when she was little, so they're really old. I like them a lot though.

KYLIE. Thanks, Gunther.

GUNTHER. That's not my name!

KYLIE. *(gently)* Well, can I call you that? It sounds like it's from a comic.

GUNTHER. Um…I guess.

KYLIE. Ok.

GUNTHER. *(He stands behind KYLIE and opens the comic book for her, then he points.)* I like this issue. Aquaman saves Antboy from drowning and Antboy becomes the best sidekick in superhero history.

KYLIE. *(looking at all the magazines on the sidewalk)* Have you read all of these?

GUNTHER. Yeah. I have a whole bunch more. Miss Nanny collected every one.

KYLIE. Wow.

(*KYLIE hands him back his magazine.*)

GUNTHER. *(pushing the magazine back to her)* You can keep it for a while.

KYLIE. Thank you.

(*KYLIE pulls her knees up to her chest. GUNTHER sits back down on the sidewalk and starts putting the comic books back into his backpack.*)

KYLIE. You probably think I'm pretty weird, don't you?

GUNTHER. No.

KYLIE. Why am I still talking to you?

GUNTHER. Maybe you like me.

KYLIE. *(laughs)* Yeah, maybe. *(a beat)* Do your parents know where you are?

GUNTHER. Well, I'm sure my mom wouldn't mind.

KYLIE. What about your dad?

GUNTHER. I don't know him.

KYLIE. How come?

GUNTHER. My parents are divorced.

KYLIE. Yeah. Mine too. *(pause)* Where are you supposed to be right now?

GUNTHER. *(sighs)* I dunno.

KYLIE. Where does your mom expect you to be?

GUNTHER. Playing basketball at summer school.

KYLIE. And why aren't you?

GUNTHER. Because it's stupid! Everyone else is bigger than me and they always shove me and call me a baby.

KYLIE. So you ran away?

GUNTHER. I walked away.

KYLIE. But you gave up?

GUNTHER. No! I just didn't feel like playing any-moreeeeeeeeee. *(He yells.)*

KYLIE. Whoa.

> (**GUNTHER** *sits, fuming.* **KYLIE** *is rather taken aback with his fit. There's a silence.)*

KYLIE. You shouldn't let people bully you.

GUNTHER. How would you know? Have you ever been picked on?

KYLIE. One time too many.

GUNTHER. What did you do?

KYLIE. Well, nothing I guess.

GUNTHER. And you're mad at me?

KYLIE. It's a lot easier in theory than in practice, ok? Look Gunther, you should probably be heading home.

GUNTHER. But it's getting dark.

KYLIE. So what do you want me to do about it? Screw in a new light bulb?

GUNTHER. You are kinda weird.

KYLIE. *(stands up and puts her hands on her hips)* Your point?

GUNTHER. Do I have to have one?

KYLIE. I guess not. *(She stretches out her hand to him.)* Come on, get up.

GUNTHER. Why?

KYLIE. Becccaauussssee…Since it's dark and you're scared, I'm going to walk you home.

GUNTHER. I'm not scared!

KYLIE. Well, since you know where I live, I should know where you live, right? It's only fair.

*(**GUNTHER** grumbles something inaudible as he gets up without help from **KYLIE***'s hand, which she promptly drops after seeing he doesn't need assistance.)*

KYLIE. *(cont.) (stepping off the curb of the sidewalk)* Which direction?

*(**GUNTHER** points.)*

Ok, come on.

GUNTHER. You have to hold hands and look both ways before crossing the street.

KYLIE. You've been programmed well.

*(**GUNTHER** sticks his hand out to **KYLIE** who reluctantly takes it.)*

KYLIE. Better?

GUNTHER. Mmmhmm.

(They walk off the stage.)

Scene Four

*(**KYLIE** is in her closet with a phone, the stuffed octopus, and her box of collected items. She pauses a moment before dialing.)*

KYLIE. *(on the phone)* Hi Jed.

> *(Lights up on* **JED**, *Kylie's 19 year-old brother as he answers the phone.)*

JED. Kylie, I called you four times this week!

KYLIE. Sorry, I didn't know. The phones have been off for a while. I just got them on again yesterday.

JED. Did your mom not pay the bills?

KYLIE. She's your mom too.

JED. Uh-huh. So how's the job going?

KYLIE. No, um, well don't be mad but…I quit.

JED. What?! Why?

KYLIE. I don't know Jed, I just did.

JED. Kylie, would you stop messing around. There aren't many places in town that are going to hire a purple haired teenager.

KYLIE. Well at least I didn't just up and leave.

> *(She hangs up. The phone promptly starts to ring.)*

KYLIE. What?

JED. Enough with the temperamental. Are you going to get another job?

KYLIE. I'm looking.

JED. Do you have enough money for the plane ticket yet?

KYLIE. Almost, but not enough to help you with rent.

JED. I told you not to worry about that Kylie, as long as you can get the plane ticket I can get the rest.

KYLIE. Well, I'll be out there by the end of the summer.

JED. Yeah, that's what you said about the end of fall and then spring and –

KYLIE. I'm trying, ok?

JED. Look, I really want you to come out. You'd like the city, and I could take you to my gigs. There aren't many yet, but we're putting together a demo. The parks are really are nice, there's some pretty cool theaters you'd like, and the food's great. Not to mention…Kylie?

KYLIE. I'm here.

JED. *(a beat)* I had to leave.

(no answer)

There's nothing for me there. And I couldn't keep living at home forever, Mom, everything. I needed my space.

KYLIE. Yeah.

I feel…guilty. I can't just leave her.

JED. *(frustrated)* I thought we talked about this already –

KYLIE. Everyone leaves her, it's not fair.

JED. Kylie –

KYLIE. What's she going to do by herself? She already drinks to the point of passing out –

JED. Do you really want to stay?

KYLIE. No, I just… I don't know.

JED. It's not healthy for you to be emotionally used every time she's depressed.

(pause)

Look, I would've taken you with me but I didn't know where I was going and then I got involved in a band, and I never meant for you to be stuck there for so long.

KYLIE. Whatever.

JED. But when you get out here, everything's gonna be just like we said all right? It'll be great. I'll look after you and we'll go on 3:00 am adventures running through the city…

KYLIE. And stay up all night until the bakery opens and we get fresh bread?

JED. Yep, or like the time we broke into our old elementary school and played hopscotch…

KYLIE. Or when we put up Christmas lights in the middle of July?

JED. Or when we dressed up like grim reapers and tried to hand out candy to kids in the playground…just like that.

KYLIE. Yeah, that last one nearly got you arrested.

JED. Ok, but you know what I mean.

KYLIE. Yeah.

JED. You want me to help you look for a new job?

KYLIE. Thanks but I think I have to go do homework, ok?

JED. Isn't school out yet?

KYLIE. No, tomorrow's the last day.

JED. And you still have homework?

(There's no answer.)

JED. Well, don't forget to eat dinner.

KYLIE. Are you gonna come and tuck me in bed, too?

JED. No. Hey, did you consider babysitting?

KYLIE. Are you kidding?

JED. No, not really. You could make a load of money.

KYLIE. Along with every 12 year-old in town. I'm not the babysitting type.

JED. Maybe if you didn't have purple hair –

KYLIE. It's not anymore actually.

JED. Great, what now, green?

KYLIE. Pink actually. And just highlights.

JED. Wonderful.

KYLIE. All right, I'll *consider* babysitting if you stop being so asinine about my hair.

JED. Fine by me.

KYLIE. Fine. Bye.

JED. Bye, Kylie. Don't forget dinner and –

*(**KYLIE** hangs up. She takes a picture of Jed from her wall and puts into her box of collections, then shuts the lid.)*

Scene Five

*(**KYLIE** is standing at the door to the Hunter's house. She looks at the scrap of paper she's holding and then rings the doorbell. The **GRANDMA** answers. She's an older woman dressed in a man's button-up tie-dye shirt and jeans.)*

KYLIE. *(nervously)* Hi, I'm Kylie Fielder. Um…Is this the Hunter residence?

GRANDMA. Yes.

KYLIE. Is Mrs. Hunter here?

GRANDMA. Yes.

KYLIE. I came in reply to an ad about a babysitter.

GRANDMA. We don't have one.

KYLIE. That's why I'm here.

GRANDMA. Not following.

KYLIE. You wanted a babysitter. Last night, I spoke with someone on the phone, I was supposed to come for an interview this morning.

(Pause. The **GRANDMA** *eyes* **KYLIE.***)*

GRANDMA. How old are you?

KYLIE. 16, like I said last night…You're Mrs. Hunter?

GRANDMA. So what are your qualifications?

KYLIE. Pardon?

GRANDMA. *(slowly and loudly as if Kylie can't hear correctly)* Qual-i-fi-ca-tions. You know, what experiences you've had?

KYLIE. Work, or as a babysitter?

GRANDMA. Both.

KYLIE. For babysitting, we used to have a neighbor and I babysat for her little girl for about three years. They just moved four months ago. I worked at the grocery store Stater Brother's…for a while. I've done a small amount of secretarial stuff. I –

GRANDMA. No, no, no! I mean experience with learning disorders, with Autism.

KYLIE. What?!

GRANDMA. Do you have any?

KYLIE. Learning disorders?

GRANDMA. Experience with handling such things.

KYLIE. *(panicking)* I didn't know I was supposed to.

GRANDMA. She didn't tell you?

KYLIE. Who's "she?"

GRANDMA. My daughter, Emma Hunter.

KYLIE. I'm sorry. I'm kind of confused.

GRANDMA. I'm the Grandma, Miss Endon. The child you want to baby-sit has autism. Didn't know, right?

KYLIE. No.

GRANDMA. Well I'm very sorry to inform you that you are simply too inexperienced and too young. The position has been filled already. Thank you and good-bye.

(*The* **GRANDMA** *is about to shut the door when someone from offstage calls to her.*)

MRS. HUNTER. Who's at the door?

GRANDMA. Some teenager selling something we don't need.

(**KYLIE** *gives her a strange look and then* **MRS. HUNTER** *appears in the doorway next to the* **GRANDMA**.)

MRS. HUNTER. What? (*realizing* **KYLIE** *is present*) Oh! Hello.

(*Looking from* **KYLIE** *to the* **GRANDMA** *for an explanation or an introduction. She notices no one is going to say anything and then proceeds.*)

MRS. HUNTER. I don't think we've met. (*She extends her hand.*) I'm Emma Hunter.

KYLIE. (*taking* **MRS. HUNTER***'s hand*) Hi, I'm Kylie Fielder.

MRS. HUNTER. You're the one I talked to last night?

KYLIE. Yes.

MRS. HUNTER. Oh, I'm sorry, if I had known you were here I would have come to talk with you. Do you still have time?

KYLIE. I thought the position had been filled.

MRS. HUNTER. Noooo… (*She looks at the* **GRANDMA**.) Why don't you go check on Guthrie for a bit while I talk with Miss Fielder? He's in the middle of an art project and shouldn't be alone with scissors for too long.

GRANDMA. He shouldn't be left with scissors at all Emma.

> *(The **GRANDMA** exits.)*

MRS. HUNTER. *(to **KYLIE**)* Come in please.

> **(KYLIE** *enters into a dinning room with a small table and several chairs. Both she and **MRS. HUNTER** take a seat.)*

MRS. HUNTER. Right. Well, did she tell you about Guthrie's condition?

KYLIE. Yes.

MRS. HUNTER. *(Sighs and sits down.)* Are you still interested in babysitting? I understand if you aren't.

KYLIE. But…what – I'm so confused.

MRS. HUNTER. Here, don't worry. I'll explain from the beginning. I need someone to look after Guthrie, my son, while I work. I'm an accountant and have set up my office at home. Basically I need someone to watch Guthrie and play with him while I can't.

KYLIE. So you don't need someone who works with learning disorders?

MRS. HUNTER. No, no. I take him into the city for that… My mother and I are both very, very stressed from our recent move here, and the transition of getting Guthrie into a school that deals with his learning needs. I apologize for not telling you all of this on the phone yesterday, but it was a very hectic evening. I also find I can concentrate better when I talk to someone in person.

KYLIE. So what kind "qualifications" are you looking for then?

MRS. HUNTER. Well, a large amount of patience is essential. So is an interest in children, the ability to keep Guthrie amused, and the common sense to come get me if something goes wrong.

KYLIE. I think I can do that.

MRS. HUNTER. Good. Now what do you know about Autism?

KYLIE. It's a disorder …of…um…the…

MRS. HUNTER. It's a developmental disorder of the brain. There is a wide spectrum of symptoms and the way it affects each individual varies greatly. Guthrie prefers when things are neat, ordered, and organized, he becomes infatuated with certain toys or words for a while, but then one day if you mention it, whatever the object or thing is will make him upset. If he starts getting quiet and red in the face come get me immediately. He has pretty overwhelming temper tantrums, his emotions and senses are sometimes too much for him to control so he might throw things, but mostly he'll scream. Most of the time though he's really very gentle, and very sensitive.

KYLIE. Anything in particular to avoid?

MRS. HUNTER. Don't go anywhere near sidewalk chalk.

KYLIE. Ok…

MRS. HUNTER. Guthrie's a sweet, bright boy. I know it must sound terrifying to you. I've been trying more and more to get him involved into social situations so I think it would be nice for him to be looked after by some one a little younger than the typical nanny or caretaker. Do you have any more questions?

KYLIE. What exactly do you want me to do?

MRS. HUNTER. Read to him or play with him. We have legos, books, toy cars, action figures, cards, all of it. He likes to talk a lot, so I figure if you listen to his stories that would be fine.

KYLIE. How long each day?

MRS. HUNTER. About four hours.

KYLIE. What do I do if he gets hungry?

MRS. HUNTER. It's probably best to come get me. He's very picky about his foods. Does all this sound reasonable?

KYLIE. Uh, I think so.

MRS. HUNTER. And you enjoy working with children?

KYLIE. Yes…lots.

MRS. HUNTER. Wonderful. I'm certainly willing to give it a try.

KYLIE. *(hesitantly)* Yeah. I'm not sure…

MRS. HUNTER. I can pay fifteen dollars an hour.

KYLIE. Ok.

MRS. HUNTER. I'll phone to arrange a time for you to start. When are you available again?

KYLIE. Whenever.

MRS. HUNTER. Excellent. Then I'll be right back to introduce you to Guthrie.

(**MRS. HUNTER** *exits and* **KYLIE** *looks around, still in shock.* **MRS. HUNTER** *re-enters with* **GUNTHER** *in tow.* **KYLIE***'s glee rapidly fades and* **GUNTHER**, *who entered solemnly, now looks thrilled.*)

MRS. HUNTER. Guthrie, this is…

(**GUNTHER** *runs up to* **KYLIE** *excitedly.*)

GUNTHER. *(screaming in excitement)* KyRieeeeeee!!!!!

KYLIE. Gunther…

MRS. HUNTER. You've met?

(**KYLIE** *barely suppresses a groan.* **GUNTHER** *is looking back and forth between* **MRS. HUNTER** *and* **KYLIE** *with a very large smile on his face.*)

KYLIE. Not really, just…

GUNTHER. Yeah, I talk to Kyrie all the time. She brought me back to the corner. She wanted to take me home, but Miss Nanny told me not to show strangers where I live…

MRS. HUNTER. That afternoon when you were supposed to be playing basketball at your camp?

(**GUNTHER** *is silent.*)

MRS. HUNTER. I see. *(turning to* **KYLIE***)* I should thank you profusely. I was panicking, and actually it's one of the reasons I'm looking for a babysitter. They said it was a well-supervised program for special needs children, but…well, thank you.

KYLIE. It really wasn't any big deal.

MRS. HUNTER. Well I'm glad you've met! *(turning to* **KYLIE***)* I'm sorry, did you call him, uh…Gunther?

KYLIE. Yeah. That's what he told me his name was.

GUNTHER. *(with indignation)* I DID NOT!!!

MRS. HUNTER. Shh-shh. It's ok. I think it's very cute; it sounds like a name from the comics. *(to* **KYLIE***)* It was nice meeting you. And thank you again. I'll call you soon.

KYLIE. All right, thank you.

GUNTHER. Bye Kyrie!

KYLIE. Uh…bye.

*(***KYLIE*** exits.)*

*(***MRS. HUNTER*** sits down and turns to* **GUNTHER***.)*

MRS. HUNTER. What do you think?

GUNTHER. You want *her* to baby-sit me?

MRS. HUNTER. I was thinking of it.

GUNTHER. *(shrugs)* Sure.

Scene Six

(The **GRANDMA** *and* **GUNTHER** *are sitting by a little kids' inflatable play pool. The* **GRANDMA** *is trying to convince* **GUNTHER** *to go in the water.)*

GRANDMA. Don't you want to go in Guthrie?

*(***GUNTHER*** shakes his head.)*

Aren't you hot? It's 90 degrees out.

*(***GUNTHER*** nods.)*

Then why not go in the water?

GUNTHER. I don't like it.

GRANDMA. Why not?

GUNTHER. It's not water, Miss Nanny.

GRANDMA. It comes from a hose. A hose that is part of the water line that runs through our house. You drink this water, you bathe in this water, why can't you play in this water? And why can't you call me "Grandma?"

(**GUNTHER** *is silent.* **KYLIE** *enters.*)

GUNTHER. *(screaming in joy)* KyRie!!!

KYLIE. *(wincing)* Hi Gunther.

GRANDMA. Gunther?

KYLIE. Yeah, it's a nickname…Mrs. Hunter asked me to baby-sit.

GRANDMA. I can care for Guthrie today.

KYLIE. Oh. Mrs. Hunter said you were going into town.

GRANDMA. I decided to take Guthrie with me.

GUNTHER. It's ok, I'll stay with Kyrie.

GRANDMA. Are you sure?

GUNTHER. *(shrugs)* I don't want to go anywhere unless Kyrie goes too.

(**KYLIE** *looks back and forth between them, unsure what to do or say.*)

GRANDMA. All right. *(to **KYLIE**)* Please watch him carefully around the water.

KYLIE. We'll be careful.

GUNTHER. Bye Miss Nanny.

GRANDMA. Bye Guthrie.

(*She exits.*)

(**KYLIE** *goes over to* **GUNTHER** *who is beside the pool and sits by him.* **GUNTHER** *won't touch the water but is mesmerized by it.* **KYLIE** *however, is rolling up her pants and starts dipping her feet in the pool.*)

KYLIE. Don't you want to get in?

GUNTHER. *(shakes his head)* No, but do you want to play demons in the water and the suckers that sink?

KYLIE. Not particularly, Gunther.

GUNTHER. Why not? Acro-man wouldn't surrender.

KYLIE. Well, I guess Acro…whatever and I are different.

GUNTHER. Acro-man!!! You cursed him. Now you have to get up, spit six times, and strike an Acro-man pose.

(**GUNTHER** *demonstrates a position with one arm across his chest and the other launched into the air, making a peace sign with two fingers. He opens his eyes and lets his arms fall, then turns to* **KYLIE.**)

Your turn now.

KYLIE. *(She laughs.)* I don't think so. I'll let you do all the stunt work.

GUNTHER. No! *(He shakes her hand off of his shoulder.)* You must honor Acro-lord…

KYLIE. I thought it was Acro-man.

GUNTHER. Whatever.

KYLIE. But aren't I performing this silly stunt because I messed up the name?

GUNTHER. *(sighs)* No. Kyrie, you just have to do it. Otherwise Acro-man will get eaten by the seven monsters from the seven layers of doom and then ejected from the universe.

KYLIE. That would be tragic.

GUNTHER. But then who'll save me?

KYLIE. You will.

GUNTHER. Kyrie, pleeeaaasssseeeeeee!!!!!

(**KYLIE** *shakes her head.*)

(screaming and growing red in the face) Noooooooooooooo!

(**KYLIE** *hurries to perform the gesture. She quickly finishes; stumbling through the whole process until she clumsily sticks her arm in the air and then sits back down.*)

(looking up as if watching the weather) Acro-man must be mad at you. The clouds don't like you.

KYLIE. Why? Is Acro-man in charge of the weather?

GUNTHER. *(nodding his head and still watching the sky)* Uh-huh.

KYLIE. It does look like we're about to get a summer thunderstorm. I think Gunther that we should go inside.

GUNTHER. Good idea. *(getting up)* Bye-bye Acro-man. See you tomorrow.

*(**KYLIE** gets up. She stands, stretches, and then reaches down to unroll her jeans. As she stands back up, one of her arms hits **GUNTHER** and knocks him backwards towards the water. He struggles for a minute, trying to regain balance by waving his arms. **KYLIE** jumps into the pool and grabs him just as his arm hits the water and creates a small splash. **KYLIE** sighs, relieved, and places him on the ground as far from the pool as she can. She gets out looking rather wet and goes up to **GUN-THER**, who is just sitting, staring at the water droplets on his very pale arm. **KYLIE** worriedly watches him.)*

KYLIE. Are you ok, Gunther?

*(**GUNTHER** doesn't look at **KYLIE**, but just stares at his arm.)*

Look at me.

GUNTHER. *(Looks towards **KYLIE** with big tears in his eyes.)* You got acid drops on me.

KYLIE. *(dismissively)* It's just water. You'll be fine.

GUNTHER. *(shaking his head)* I don't think so.

KYLIE. Look. I'm all wet. I was just in the water. It doesn't hurt me. In fact, it feels good. Watch.

*(**KYLIE** goes over to the hose and splashes water on her face. **GUNTHER** starts screaming.)*

GUNTHER. Don't do that.

KYLIE. It's water!

*(**GUNTHER** is amazed by **KYLIE**. After a moment, he looks at her pleadingly and the tears return.)*

GUNTHER. Kyrie…I'm not going to die, am I?

KYLIE. *(laughing)* Of course not. I'm fine.

GUNTHER. But you're a superhero…even better than Acro-man.

KYLIE. No, Gunther I'm not your superman. I can be broken into tiny pieces, just like everyone else.

GUNTHER. But you're…you're…superwoman.

KYLIE. *(shakes her head slowly)* No, I'm just Kylie. Watch. I'll show you that the water can't hurt you either.

> (**KYLIE** *goes over to the pool and cups her hands and fills them with water. She goes to* **GUNTHER,** *who recoils, places his hands over his eyes, but still peeks out to see what* **KYLIE** *is doing. She tips her hands so that one drop of water slowly falls onto his arm.* **GUNTHER** *watches it slide on his skin for a moment, then starts to breathe faster and faster. His face is full of anguish.* **KYLIE** *doesn't seem to notice and laughs.)*

> See?

GUNTHER. *(begins to howl)* Owwww! Ow! Ow! It's hurting Kyrie, it's hurting.

KYLIE. Don't be silly, you were fine a second ago.

GUNTHER. Help me!

KYLIE. Stop it Gunther.

GUNTHER. *(begins to cry and plead in a quiet voice)* Please Kyrie, please.

> (**KYLIE** *dries him with a shirt. She is dripping, but tries not to get anything on* **GUNTHER.** **GUNTHER** *stares in front of him, shocked.)*

GUNTHER. *(cont.)* *(tears slowly dripping down his cheeks)* Kyrie, you hurt me.

> (**GUNTHER** *gets up dejectedly and walks away from* **KYLIE.***)*

KYLIE. Gunther, where are you going?

GUNTHER. Away!!

KYLIE. Why?

GUNTHER. Because you're not my friend anymore.

> (**GUNTHER** *stops walking and* **KYLIE** *goes up to him.)*

KYLIE. I just wanted to help you Gunther, not to injure you.

GUNTHER. But I don't like water and you put it on me.

KYLIE. I was trying to show you'd be fine.

GUNTHER. *(insistently)* But I wasn't.

KYLIE. Weren't you?

(**GUNTHER** *shakes his head.*)

GUNTHER. You're supposed to be the one who protects me.

KYLIE. I guess I messed up. Will you forgive me?

GUNTHER. Will you put water all over me again?

KYLIE. Never.

GUNTHER. Swear on Acro-man?

KYLIE. I swear in the mighty Acro-man's hallowed name.

(**GUNTHER** *looks at her for a moment, then nods.*)
Are we friends again?

(**GUNTHER** *nods for a second time.*)
Someone once told me that when they feel bad it's helpful to read comics. What do you say we try that?

GUNTHER. *(sighing)* It's not just any comics, they're Aquaman comics. I have to show you my whole collection. Come on.

KYLIE. Ok.

(**GUNTHER** *jumps up and runs offstage.* **KYLIE** *quickly follows him.*)

Scene Seven

(**KYLIE** *sits in the living room, reading a magazine and smoking. Her* **MOTHER** *enters, behind in the kitchen area, looks in the fridge.*)

KYLIE. *(sarcastic)* Welcome back. Where you been?

MOM. Out.

KYLIE. Really, I didn't notice.

MOM. Running errands. Some stuff. Nothing important.

KYLIE. Don't you wonder why it's never you asking me that?

MOM. Asking what?

KYLIE. Never mind.

(**MOTHER** *grabs the pickle jar and starts eating out of it.*)

MOM. Do you think you could pick up ground beef tonight, I was thinking of making spaghetti?

KYLIE. One, you never cook. Two, no.

MOM. Why not? You work at a grocery store.

KYLIE. Not anymore.

MOM. What? Why not?

KYLIE. I dunno. How come you don't work at St. Andrews anymore? Or the diner? Or the bank? Or the gallery?

MOM. All right enough, I'm not taking that right now.

KYLIE. All right, neither am I.

MOM. You wanna be grounded Kylie?

KYLIE. Definitely.

MOM. And where did you get those cigarettes? I thought we talked about that already.

KYLIE. You left them on the counter. Leave the knives out, the kids'll play with them.

MOM. Since when did you know so much about it?

KYLIE. Ever since you didn't.

MOM. For gods sake Kylie! Go to your room.

KYLIE. It's too hot in there.

MOM. Then smarten up or that won't be my problem. *(a beat)* What do you want for dinner?

KYLIE. As long as it's of greater quality than Taco Bell or twinkies I really don't care.

MOM. That was once and I was having a bad day.

KYLIE. Whatever. I might not be back anyways.

MOM. Well then, no one will be complaining about burrito supreme.

KYLIE. Don't you want to know where I'm gonna be?

MOM. I'd assume you'd tell me if you were going to, or not tell me if you weren't. You're generally responsible so I assume you'll be fine. I'm not expecting to get a call that you're spray painting anarchy signs in the graveyard, in other words, you aren't your brother. Jed, I would ask, but –

(She stops herself. Goes back to the fridge and puts the pickles back. Doesn't look at KYLIE.)

If you could pick up some coffee I'd appreciate it. We're almost out.

(*There's no response from* **KYLIE**.)

I'm going to work.

KYLIE. Fine.

(**MOM** *exits.*)

Bye Mom…

(**KYLIE** *puts out the cigarette. She picks up the phone and calls* **JED**.)

Hey.

(*lights up on* **JED** *working at a pizza stand.*)

JED. Yo. What's going on?

KYLIE. I dunno. Just wanted to call.

JED. Ok. (*pause*) How are you?

KYLIE. Fine.

JED. Hmm. Wanna hear something interesting?

KYLIE. Sure.

JED. (*off phone to customers*) No, you need to put those down. I'm sorry.

KYLIE. What?

JED. (*still off the phone*) No, we're out. I can take your order when you're ready. Two cheese and a… (*back on phone*) Sorry. I'm at work.

KYLIE. Yeah, I could hear.

JED. Anyway, I was gonna tell you about this new record store that's apparently moving in down the street from me.

KYLIE. Uh huh.

JED. You sure you're ok?

KYLIE. Yeah, of course.

JED. All right. Anyway, it's the same guy who owned the tattoo shop there, don't know what he –
(*off phone*) No, it won't be ready for another 5 minutes. You want a soda? Which size? Sure thing.
(*on phone*) Hold on a sec. (*pause*) Ok, you still there?

KYLIE. Yeah, but if you need to go back to work…

JED. No worries. Ronny will cover for me. You've got 2 minutes kiddo, shoot.

KYLIE. It's really nothing.

JED. Bullshit. Mom. Go.

KYLIE. It's just I told her I was going out and she didn't seem to care.

JED. Yeah, most kids your age don't complain about that.

KYLIE. She never notices me Jed, except when she needs favors or a punching bag.

JED. Yep. That's Mom. Where are you going anyways?

KYLIE. I dunno. Probably just to the shore to go sulk until an unreasonable hour when I'll wander home and slam the door to see if she wakes up from the couch coma and if not I'll go sulk some more in my bedroom.

JED. Sounds pretty melodramatic.

KYLIE. Do you have a better idea?

JED. Yeah. Goes like this: buy a calendar, cross off days till the 26th of August when you're going to be out here. A real date and a real time to stick to. Deal?

(no reponse)

Deal Kylie?

KYLIE. Right then. Deal.

JED. Ok, I've got to get back to work, but call tonight or tomorrow if you need anything.

KYLIE. Yeah. Thanks.

JED. Don't mention it.

> *(They hang up. **KYLIE** pulls out another cigarette, holds it in her mouth without lighting it. From under the coffee table she pulls out her shoebox and looks at some of the objects. Inspired, she dumps out the box and starts arranging objects on the sofa like a collage.)*

Scene Eight

(**KYLIE** *and* **GUNTHER** *are in the Hunter's living room.* **GUNTHER** *is playing with* **KYLIE***'s stuffed octopus.*)

KYLIE. Having fun, Gunther?

GUNTHER. Yeah. Seven flying spaceships are attacking Cheetah. I have to help him find a place to hide before it's too late.

(**GUNTHER** *waves the stuffed octopus while making zooming and swooshing sound effects.*)

KYLIE. You named my name octopus "Cheetah?"

GUNTHER. Did you have a name for him?

KYLIE. I'd rather not expose the embarrassing layers of my 4 year-old psyche thanks.

(**GUNTHER** *looks at her.*)

That's a no.

GUNTHER. *(shrugs)* Then Cheetah's just his name. It's what the Intergalactic Space Federation of Naming, Births, and Deaths decided to call him. It's probably because of how fast he is.

KYLIE. How fast?

GUNTHER. Like nothing you've ever seen. He's the best from our galaxy and second from everywhere else.

KYLIE. Who's first?

GUNTHER. The evil Pirating and Slave Trading Company's captain. His name's Snail.

KYLIE. But I thought he was the fastest.

GUNTHER. He is in speed, but he thinks a decade slower than you and me. That's why Cheetah always captures him. Did you know that it took Snail an entire year for him to learn how to tie his shoes? It took me only a month.

KYLIE. He's not very bright I guess.

GUNTHER. Nope. But Cheetah is. He beat the whole space fleet to their head quarters, *and* rescued all the prisoners before the generals even knew what was going on. Did you know Cheetah has so many medals of honor that he has an extra house for them?

KYLIE. No, I definitely didn't.

GUNTHER. He's that good.

KYLIE. Did you read all this stuff in a comic?

GUNTHER. *(laughs)* No Kyrie. This is real.

> (**GUNTHER** *sticks the octopus under the sofa quickly and indicates that* **KYLIE** *should be quiet.*)

KYLIE. What's…

GUNTHER. Shhh!

> (**GUNTHER** *checks both directions and then turns to* **KYLIE.**)

Sorry, I had to make sure that he had outrun them by a few light years.

KYLIE. Oh.

GUNTHER. Do you want to do something else while we wait for those years to pass?

KYLIE. Sure, what do you want to do?

GUNTHER. *(shrugs)* We could dress up like pirates.

> (**GUNTHER** *heads over to a big purple bucket that holds clothes for dressing up.* **KYLIE** *follows him and looks into the bucket. She pulls out a purple vest and measures it against* **GUNTHER.**)

KYLIE. I think you need this.

GUNTHER. Ok. I need a hat, too.

> (*They rummage in the bin for a while until* **KYLIE** *pulls out a squished-looking brown cowboy hat.*)

KYLIE. Well, this could work…

GUNTHER. I suppose I could be a cowboy-pirate.

KYLIE. *(putting the hat on him)* It works.

GUNTHER. *(pulling out a plastic sword)* I'll definitely be needing this.

KYLIE. But never to use except as a last resort to do good, right?

GUNTHER. Of course! And never on women or children or nice men, only on evil aliens who are mean and cruel.

KYLIE. Right then. You know, I'm not sure about pirates, but I know knights go through a ceremony of being knighted. *(She shrugs).* I suppose you could always be a pirate-cowboy-knight.

GUNTHER. Ok. Then you have to knight me. But first we should dress you up.

*(They dig through the bin some more and **KYLIE** pulls out a witch hat. She puts it on and shows it to **GUN-THER**, but he shakes his head and replaces it with a crown. He shakes his head again and takes that off too.)*

Do you still have those wings that you wore for your play?

KYLIE. Yeah, why?

GUNTHER. Put those on.

*(**KYLIE** goes to her bag and pulls out the crumpled look-ing wings and puts them on.)*

GUNTHER. Good.

KYLIE. *(trying to examine herself)* Exactly what kind of pirate am I supposed to be?

GUNTHER. *(as if it's obvious)* A Kyrie-fairy one. Ok, now knight me. Wait! *(He jumps up, runs to the sofa, and grabs Cheetah.)* Cheetah wants to be a knight too.

KYLIE. Right then.

*(**GUNTHER** kneels and holds his stuffed octopus beside him.)*

I proclaim you Gunther, the pirate-cowboy, a knight of the Royal Empire of this galaxy. And you Cheetah…

*(She brings the fake sword over to the octopus but acci-dentally knocks it out of **GUNTHER**'s hands. She bends down to pick it up but drops the sword on top of it.)*

Whoops. Sorry.

GUNTHER. *(staring in shock)* You killed him, Kyrie.

KYLIE. *(picking up the octopus and sword)* It doesn't look very dead to me, Gunther.

GUNTHER. *(taking the octopus from her and inspecting it)* Yep, he's a goner.

KYLIE. But…I…Gunther, I've had him since I was two and he's been through a lot more. I'm sure he's fine.

GUNTHER. Nope.

(pause)

That's all right; we can have a funeral for him.

KYLIE. A what?!

GUNTHER. I've always wanted to see what one looks like anyways.

KYLIE. You're sick and morbid, Gunther!

GUNTHER. *(shrugs)* Do you still have that shoebox thing you were collecting stuff in? We could use it as a coffin.

KYLIE. You're really serious about this aren't you?

GUNTHER. Uh huh. Could I have it?

KYLIE. Um…no.

GUNTHER. Kyrie!!! Please!

*(**KYLIE** shakes her head.)*

GUNTHER. Fine. I'll get a towel instead.

*(**GUNTHER** exits **KYLIE** picks up octopus.)*

KYLIE. *(looking at the octopus)* I'm sorry, I didn't realize how far this would go.

*(**GUNTHER** returns with a small cloth.)*

GUNTHER. This is all I could find. You surreee we can't use the shoe-box? You owe it to Cheetah.

KYLIE. Ok, fine!

*(She digs in her bag and pulls out a shoebox. She hesitantly empties the contents and gives the box to **GUN-THER.**)*

GUNTHER. It was nice knowing you, Cheetah.

(**GUNTHER** *starts to walk out of the room but notices* **KYLIE** *isn't following him.*)

GUNTHER. Are you coming?

KYLIE. Where?

GUNTHER. To have a burial outside under his favorite oak tree.

KYLIE. How do you know where his favorite oak tree is?

GUNTHER. *(sighs)* We talked, Kylie. You coming to bury him now?

KYLIE. *(rolling her eyes)* I guess.

(*They exit with* **GUNTHER** *carrying the box and humming a funeral march.*)

Scene Nine

(**KYLIE** *enters a room where the* **GRANDMA** *is sitting on an armchair with a magazine in her lap, a vacant expression on her face.*)

KYLIE. *(calling out)* Mrs. Hunter?

(no reply)

KYLIE. Mrs. Hu… *(She notices the* **GRANDMA.***)* Hello.

GRANDMA. Emma went upstairs. Can I help you?

KYLIE. Gunther's asleep and I have to go home.

GRANDMA. Ah.

(pause)

KYLIE. Look, Miss Endon, about the other day…don't take it personally. I'm just here babysitting Gunther.

GRANDMA. *(laughs)* Hah!

KYLIE. Well, it's not like I'm trying to steal your place or anything.

GRANDMA. *(Looks at* **KYLIE** *for a moment, then frowns.)* Maybe you're right.

KYLIE. Yeah, it's just my summer job.

GRANDMA. *(Nodding, she starts speaking in a dreamy, slurred voice.)* You know what, it's true. *(She cocks her head in thought.)* They've already replaced me. A long time ago. It's just me…realizing it now.

KYLIE. That's not what I meant!!

GRANDMA. *(still dreamy)* No, no, that's what I meant. You see, when you're old like me, your job is replaceable. Life is a failed sinecure where you do nothing, get to be nothing, and get rewarded with nothing. The song keeps playing without you. You're an extra note to get rid of.

KYLIE. I'm really sure that that's not how anyone feels about you.

GRANDMA. Everyone is waiting for the last breath to be drawn.

KYLIE. What are you talking about?!

GRANDMA. The end…the place where none of us wants to go. The place where they want me. They're calling.

KYLIE. *(in utter confusion)* Why are we even discussing this?

GRANDMA. Don't bother yourself with the old, child. Be happy with the new.

KYLIE. You aren't making any sense.

> (**KYLIE** *spots a bottle of vodka at the Grandma's feet.*)

GRANDMA. You can never drink too much life. It fills you, but you want to keep going, keep going, until…the end…

*(The **GRANDMA** rests her head on the back of her armchair, and then turns her head.)*

Good night, the pie was excellent. *(She starts singing, drunkenly.)* "I ain't lookin to compete with you, beat or cheat or mistreat you, simplify, classify, deny, defy or crucify you. All IIII really wanna dooooooo, is baby be friends with you…" *(sighs)* It's all right that you don't like me. You'll see the way in the end. But right now I…I have to…

(She appears to have fallen asleep, and **KYLIE** *is shaking her head and waving her arms in frustration. She leans in as if trying to hear if there was going to be something more, something logical. The* **GRANDMA** *snores and* **KYLIE** *jumps and stands straight again.)*

KYLIE. Right then. That made so much sense. *(to no one in particular)* See you on Monday.

*(***KYLIE** *exits.)*

Scene Ten

*(***KYLIE** *and* **GUNTHER** *are in the driveway in front of* **GUNTHER***'s house.* **GUNTHER** *is practicing shooting hoops, but keeps missing.* **KYLIE** *is sitting on the ground with her arms crossed, staring at* **GUNTHER***.)*

GUNTHER. This sucks. I don't see why I have to do this.

KYLIE. *(looks up)* You're the one that said you're terrible at basketball. You're not going to get better by whining about it. You have to get better by practicing.

*(***GUNTHER** *tries again but misses.)*

GUNTHER. Why am I so bad at this?

KYLIE. Hmmm…Because your hand –

GUNTHER. And eye coordination sucks. Yeah. I know. *(He sits down on the ground and throws the basketball.)* I hate basketball.

KYLIE. I promised you I'd help you learn, but I never promised it would be easy. You can't just expect that basketball or anything else will come naturally. If you just do what's easy, then you're avoiding anything that you have to work for. And if you work for something Gunther, it will reward you more than if you just get it out of sheer luck or talent. You'll feel proud of yourself and your accomplishment. Basketball is something –

GUNTHER. *(grumbling)* Don't even say that word.

(**KYLIE** *goes over to him and squats down beside him.*)

KYLIE. Gunther, don't get mad at yourself for missing; just keep trying. This is something that you need to conquer. You have to be persistent.

GUNTHER. Everyone else is better than me.

KYLIE. That's because they've had more practice than you. The ones who haven't probably have advantages like size. But when you're their height, you'll be the one who's practiced and they won't. Be patient.

GUNTHER. I hate being short.

KYLIE. You're missing the point. Basketball isn't –

GUNTHER. Don't say that word!!!!!

KYLIE. Come on. Pick on the ball and –

GUNTHER. *(screaming)* Don't say that!!! (*He puts his hands on his ears and starts screeching.*)

KYLIE. Stop it. Gunther, stop it!

(**GUNTHER** *lies on the ground and starts banging his fists.*)

GUNTHER. I don't want to, I don't want to!!! Let me be. It's not fair! Don't do thatttttttttttttttttt!!!!

(**GUNTHER** *picks up the little pieces of gravel in the driveway and starts throwing them at* **KYLIE.** *She stands up and backs away.*)

Go away! Go away!

(**KYLIE** *walks closer to* **GUNTHER,** *covering her face. She tries to grab hold of his fists. She manages for a minute but* **GUNTHER** *starts kicking.*)

LET ME GO!!! LET GO!!

(*They wrestle for a minute but* **KYLIE** *finally lets go, panting.* **GUNTHER** *is still screaming.* **KYLIE** *exits and then returns with* **MRS. HUNTER. MRS. HUNTER** *slowly goes up to the screaming* **GUNTHER** *and gently places a hand on his back.*)

MRS. HUNTER. Guthrie?

*(The **GRANDMA** enters and looks at the screaming **GUN-THER**, **KYLIE**, and **MRS. HUNTER**. She walks up, nods to **MRS. HUNTER** and she picks up **GUNTHER**'s arms while **MRS. HUNTER** picks up his legs. They carry him, thrashing, offstage. **KYLIE** sits down again and looks worried. After a moment, the **GRANDMA** reappears and walks over to **KYLIE**.)*

GRANDMA. Are you ok?

*(**KYLIE** nods. The **GRANDMA** picks out a rock from Kylie's hair.)*

GRANDMA. *(cont.)* Did he throw the gravel at you?

*(Again **KYLIE** nods.)*

Just be glad it wasn't anything bigger. Once he started throwing his action figures at me when I was sleeping… I was bruised for –

*(**KYLIE** starts crying suddenly.)*

It's all right.

*(**KYLIE** falls onto her shoulder, and the **GRANDMA**, not sure what to do, lightly pats **KYLIE** on the back.)*

It's all right. You did ok. You didn't do anything wrong. There, there. Nothing to worry about. He'll be ok. I think you'll be ok. *(She shakes her head and then nods it.)* I know you'll be ok. *(She pauses.)* Are you ok?

*(**KYLIE** nods and starts wiping tears away from her face.)*

He didn't mean any harm just…It happens…With Guthrie, this happens.

*(**KYLIE** sighs and nods again.)*

You should probably head home. I need to see if Emma needs help.

KYLIE. *(her voice cracking)* Will he be all right?

GRANDMA. Yes.

KYLIE. I didn't mean to make him angry, I just –

GRANDMA. Don't worry. He just gets like this sometimes. But I should be getting inside…unless you want me to drive you home.

KYLIE. I think I'll walk, thanks.

GRANDMA. Ok.

KYLIE. Should I come by tomorrow?

GRANDMA. *(surprised)* You want to?

KYLIE. Yeah. I think I should.

GRANDMA. I'll uh…well…I don't know. We'll phone.

(pause)

And Kylie…I'm sorry about the other night. I was um…

KYLIE. Drunk?

GRANDMA. I was going to say very tired. Was I really drunk? I thought I just fell asleep. Did I say anything?

(KYLIE starts shaking her head and then changes it to a nod.)

What did I say? Oh, not the speech…

(KYLIE nods her head cautiously.)

Oh no. The one about life, death, birth, love, or divorce?

KYLIE. *(with uncertainty)* Um…death, I think.

GRANDMA. *(nods)* Yes. Emma hates that one. It usually puts her in tears. But not to worry. At least not for me, I don't remember what I say. *(She chuckles.)* I didn't scare you, did I?

KYLIE. I don't…um…no.

(GRANDMA bursts into a laugh. KYLIE stares at her.)

KYLIE. Do you…well, do you drink often?

GRANDMA. Oh heck, it's the cure to human emotion.

KYLIE. You need one?

GRANDMA. Oh, we all have different ones. Ignoring what bothers us, blaming it on someone else, beating ourselves up, crying, or cigarettes. We each have one, and it's all the same thing under a different name. A little escapism isn't a terrible thing. It's all about the moderation.

KYLIE. That was moderation?

GRANDMA. Well, upon careful calculations and averaging across days in a year, yes, I think it was moderation. I would say the occasional excessive behavior can help equilibrium.

(*KYLIE just looks at her.*)

Forgive the prying, but your mother…drinks?

(*KYLIE nods.*)

Often?

(*KYLIE doesn't respond.*)

GRANDMA. *(cont.)* Yes, Emma's husband too. It's hard to live with a drunk. Do me a favor and don't tell Emma about this incident of mine.

KYLIE. Will it happen again?

GRANDMA. If I told you that'd ruin all the fun wouldn't it? Oh, don't worry. It's a seldom but necessary occurrence.

KYLIE. Necessary?

GRANDMA. Yes, necessary to purge the demons, exercise the monsters, and relinquish the anxieties.

KYLIE. I see.

GRANDMA. I really should go check on Guthrie. Unless you need to talk some more, or want to come in.

KYLIE. I'm all right. But thank you.

GRANDMA. You get yourself home safe then.

KYLIE. Yeah, I'll call…

(**GRANDMA** *walks off and* **KYLIE** *stares after her.*)

Scene Eleven

(*Lights up on* **KYLIE** *in her room. She is sitting in her closet on top of boxes of toys and stuffed animals. She was writing a letter, the pen and paper now sitting on the floor as she counts money instead. She does so slowly and counts under her breath.* **KYLIE***'s mom enters.* **KYLIE** *stops counting and looks towards the door, listening to the sound of her* **MOTHER** *sighing, taking off her jacket, and sitting on the living room sofa.* **KYLIE** *flips through her money again faster, but pauses as she stares at the door in the direction of her* **MOTHER.** **KYLIE** *takes out a bag. She pulls from it a half-formed sculpture construction with objects dangling from strings. The objects are the ones we have seen* **KYLIE** *collecting throughout and the ones she arranged earlier on the sofa.* **KYLIE** *considers her creation and turns it back and forth. Lights out.)*

Scene Twelve

*(***MRS. HUNTER** *and* **KYLIE** *enter the Hunter's living room.)*

MRS. HUNTER. I'm glad you could come today.

KYLIE. No problem.

MRS. HUNTER. I'll call Guthrie down in a minute. I'm sorry about what happened the other day with his tantrum. Are you all right?

KYLIE. Yeah. Is Gunther?

MRS. HUNTER. He's better. Mostly he's not talking; he's just off in his own world. Are you sure you're up for taking care of him today?

KYLIE. I think it'll be fine.

MRS. HUNTER. I'll get him then.

(She exits and **KYLIE** *looks around.* **MRS. HUNTER** *comes back in with* **GUNTHER.** *)*

KYLIE. Hi Gunther.

MRS. HUNTER. *(to* **GUNTHER***)* You ok?

(She puts her hand affectionately on his shoulder. **GUN-THER** *shrugs off her hand and goes over to the legos.* **MRS. HUNTER** *looks at* **KYLIE** *and shakes her head.)*

MRS. HUNTER. I'll be outside if you need anything, Kylie.

(**MRS. HUNTER** *exits.*)

KYLIE. You're quiet.

(**GUNTHER** *continues silently playing with his legos.*)

It's actually kind of shocking. I'm not quite sure if it's a nice change or not. I think I was getting used to your talking.

(**KYLIE** *reaches in her bag and pulls out her sculpture.*)

I brought something to show you. Look. It's a mobile.

(**GUNTHER** *turns and stares at her.*)

KYLIE. *(cont.)* I started making it a while ago. I'm sorting of piecing everything together I guess. Remember the shoebox I was using to collect things that we buried Cheetah in? Well this is all the stuff I collected, and I tried to make something out of it. To move on. Look. Everything on here means something to me.

Like oh, that bottle. I've seen more of those lying around my house in the last few years than I care to remember. The pencil is for when my mom used to be a middle school teacher. She taught art, but left because she didn't like the administration. That was after my dad left. She's a waitress now…sometimes.

The seashell is for the time we went to Florida. Before the divorce. I didn't really know my dad. My parents separated when I was 4. He doesn't ever really talk to us anymore. I remember the beach though, and seeing dolphins. It was different from the beach here, but I'm not sure how to describe it. Warmer… This movie ticket is for the first movie I ever saw. Or so my mom says. This ticket stub though is different. It's for the fair. Not the one here. It was one in the city. It was big. I was so scared when we went up that Ferris Wheel. *(She shakes her head.)* You certainly wouldn't have thought that I was your superhero then. This is the first poem I wrote. You wouldn't like it. It's about a lake. I know… water. Anyway, I guess none of the stuff really seems all that important. For some reason it is to me. It's little bits and pieces of my life, all telling a story, and they're all here together now. I know, it's completely nostalgic, but I guess it's my version of a photo album or something. It's my memory mobile. I should put something for you on here. Would you like that? Yeah, you probably would. I'll let you do it sometime, maybe when you're feeling better. I should put something for Jed too. Even if he did leave me. *(She shrugs one shoulder.)* The good and the bad memories I guess.

*(**KYLIE** looks at **GUNTHER** who is busy building a lego city.)*

KYLIE. *(cont.)* You know, it's funny. Even when you aren't paying attention to me, I feel like you get me. You know how I feel, or at least I think you do. It seems that you're silently absorbing everything I tell you. You always understand people, even when they don't understand you. It's not really fair, is it? You probably don't mind. In fact you probably prefer it. You can read everyone else, but no one can read you. It's like you live in a different world. No one can predict you entirely. They can try, but no one will ever be sure. You'll always surprise them somehow. You always surprise me. You know what, Gunther? If I had a little brother, I hope he would be you – even if you can be obnoxious and overly talkative and weird. And you throw things at me. But that's ok. You can put up with me and I suppose I'm weirder. I'm going to miss you. I should have told you earlier about me moving I guess...

*(**KYLIE** looks over at **GUNTHER**, who has fallen asleep. **KYLIE** lifts him up and puts him on the sofa. She puts a blanket over him.)*

Good night, Gunther.

*(**KYLIE** gets her bag and heads outside where she sees **MRS. HUNTER** working on a laptop on one of the lawn chairs.)*

MRS. HUNTER. Oh hi, Kylie! Did I tell you that you don't need to baby-sit next Friday? I'm taking Guthrie up to the doctor's. There's a specialist who works on communication skills and –

KYLIE. No, you told me.

MRS. HUNTER. Do you want to sit down?

KYLIE. Uh… no…it's all right.

MRS. HUNTER. Are you ok?

KYLIE. Yeah. *(a beat)* I… I'm going away. Out to Boston.

MRS. HUNTER. Oh! How long will you be gone?

KYLIE. I'm not sure. A while. My brother's out there. I've been meaning to go for a long time.

MRS. HUNTER. I didn't know you had a brother.

KYLIE. *(silent for a moment and then blurts it out)* I'm moving.

MRS. HUNTER. Does Guthrie know?

(**KYLIE** *shakes her head.*)

KYLIE. I tried to tell him but…

MRS. HUNTER. This is awfully sudden, Kylie.

KYLIE. I know. I'm sorry.

MRS. HUNTER. I'm sure you'll be missed. Do you want to come by tomorrow and talk to Gunther?

KYLIE. I can't, I'm flying out early. It's probably better anyways. But, um, could you give him these?

(**KYLIE** *hands* **MRS. HUNTER** *the wings that* **GUNTHER** *had put on* **KYLIE**.)

MRS. HUNTER. *(nods again)* Sure.

(**MRS. HUNTER** *gives* **KYLIE** *a hug and then steps back.*)

Have a safe trip, ok?

KYLIE. I will, thanks.

MRS. HUNTER. You can phone if you like.

KYLIE. All right.

MRS. HUNTER. You can write to us, too.

KYLIE. Thanks.

MRS. HUNTER. And you can visit any time.

KYLIE. I should…go.

MRS. HUNTER. Let us know if you're ever in town and want to see Guthrie…I mean Gunther.

KYLIE. I will. Thanks.

(**KYLIE** *turns to leave and starts walking away.*)

See ya, Gunther.

Scene Thirteen

(**KYLIE** *sits at her desk, and finishes the letter she's written to her* **MOTHER.** *Her bags are already packed, and after she's finished writing, she stands, taking a last minute survey of her room. She pushes the desk chair neatly back into its place and turns out the light. Entering the living room she picks up beer bottles scattered on the coffee table and floor, placing them in a trash bag. Her* **MOTHER**'s *afghan has fallen from the back of the sofa.* **KYLIE** *reaches behind the furniture and picks it up, folding it twice and placing it over straightened pillows.* **KYLIE** *takes a moment before setting her letter on the coffee table, folded over and upright so her mom will see it right away.* **KYLIE** *exits, trash and travel bags in hand.*)

End of Scene

Scene Fourteen

(**GUNTHER** and **MRS. HUNTER** are sitting on the living room sofa together and are reading from Charlotte's Web.)

GUNTHER. Mom?

MRS. HUNTER. Yeah.

GUNTHER. When's Kyrie coming back…it's been more than a week.

MRS. HUNTER. She didn't really say. Should we write to her?

GUNTHER. Is she going to be gone a long time?

MRS. HUNTER. I don't know, but if you don't think so much about it the time will go by quickly.

(**GUNTHER** shakes his head.)

GUNTHER. It's not fair.

MRS. HUNTER. Do you want to finish reading Guthrie?

GUNTHER. No, I want Kyrie to come back, now!

MRS. HUNTER. I know. I'm sure she misses you too.

GUNTHER. She's been taken by the Super Hero Destruction Industry, hasn't she?

MRS. HUNTER. No, Guthrie. She has her own family too. And has gone to Boston to visit her brother.

GUNTHER. What if she's gone forever?

(**GUNTHER** gets red in the face and starts to cry. **GRANDMA** enters.)

GRANDMA. C'mon, Guthrie, let's go on a walk.

GUNTHER. NO! I don't want to. What did you do to Kyrie?

GRANDMA. Nothing

MRS. HUNTER. Guthrie…

GUNTHER. My name is Gunther!!

(**GUNTHER** exits and **MRS. HUNTER** and the **GRANDMA** stare after him.)

Scene Fifteen

(**KYLIE** *is sitting in* **JED** *'s apartment playing guitar. She hums then begins to play a song.* **JED** *gets up from his bed in the other room, and listens to* **KYLIE** *from the door. He starts to sing with her.*)

JED. Hey, that sounded pretty good.

KYLIE. Just because you're a rock star doesn't mean you can get up at three.

JED. Eh, why not? You like the gig last night?

KYLIE. Yeah, it was nice.

JED. Nice? Wow, we must've been really terrible. I thought it wasn't too bad myself…So what do you want to do today.

KYLIE. I dunno know.

JED. I'm up for anything but more museums.

KYLIE. Ok.

JED. Any alternatives? You must be sick of them too. There are only so many paintings on a wall you can stare at.

KYLIE. Chinatown?

JED. Uh, we had sooo much of that last week.

KYLIE. I guess. Hey, Jed? Where'd you get that wedding picture of Mom?

JED. I took it with me.

KYLIE. You mean you stole it?

JED. Well, it's not like she had them out anymore.

(*pause*)

JED. You know you look like her?

KYLIE. I'm nothing like her!

JED. I wasn't saying you were. But she has her moments.

KYLIE. I guess.

JED. Kylie, she called.

KYLIE. Oh.

JED. A few times actually.

KYLIE. When?

JED. Well, yesterday most recently.

KYLIE. And you didn't mention this because…?

JED. I am mentioning it.

KYLIE. How did she sound?

JED. Fine.

KYLIE. Fine?

JED. No, like sober fine. She really misses you. She said to apologize about something, about a lot of things, but a play…?

KYLIE. Yeah.

JED. She said you'd know what she was talking about. Anyways, you should call her. She sounded really sorry Kylie.

KYLIE. Well I'm glad.

JED. Don't be cold. She wanted to know if you're all right.

KYLIE. I'm fine and I don't want to talk about it, ok? Anyways…We could go to the commons.

JED. You, me, and Cecilia.

KYLIE. Cecilia?

JED. What? It's a pretty name for a guitar.

KYLIE. You're like those sailors who name their boats after women. One day we should get a yacht and sail around the Aleutian Islands. We could name the boat Cecilia, or Amelia, or Cordelia. In science class –

JED. Or maybe we should get you a plane ticket home on an airline called Southwest, or Delta, or Jet Blue. How do those sound?

KYLIE. What? Where did that come from?

JED. C'mon Kylie. Both of us know this isn't working.

KYLIE. What isn't?

JED. You. Here. This.

KYLIE. I've hasn't even been three weeks. Do you not want me here?

JED. No, it's good to have you.

KYLIE. Then what is this about?!

JED. You, sulking. Every day. Look, I want you to be happy. And maybe you shouldn't have left home. I just thought…just because something's right for me, doesn't mean it is for you.

KYLIE. Jed –

JED. Mom's seeing the counselor again. And she's started going to those AA meetings.

KYLIE. Yeah, but it hasn't been that long.

JED. I think you should at least talk to her.

KYLIE. Come back with me.

(JED *shakes his head.*)

I don't know. I just don't know right now.

(*pause*)

JED. Who's Gunther? Mom mentioned that he'd called you.

KYLIE. Gunther? Well, he's this kid.

JED. Care to elaborate? I thought you didn't have a boyfriend.

KYLIE. No, he's 10. C'mon.

JED. Who is he?

KYLIE. Well, you remember you suggested that I babysit? Well that's how I ended up saving the money to get here.

JED. Nice. So what kind of kid would be crazy enough to miss their punk babysitter?

KYLIE. Thanks. Actually he's autistic and he's really sweet, he has these questions. He has an amazing imagination and is full of…I dunno what you would call it, personality? You remember Cheetah? I mean my octopus? Well I gave it to Gunther and he was playing this complicated game and somehow it ended that I killed Cheetah and we had to have this burial. Gunther dug this grave three feet deep. He insisted Cheetah had to be buried with a pillow and blanket, and was going to put in a book too until I convinced him it was probably too dark down there to read. But he was sure that Cheetah would come back one day cause that's how all the stories go. He even sprinkled rice and made me build a tombstone.

JED. You miss him, huh?

KYLIE. I worry about him more than anything. I mean, he was always wandering off, and left everybody going, "Oh, where's Gunther?" But he doesn't need me there, he has a really caring mom and grandma.

JED. That missing doesn't just vanish, Kylie.

KYLIE. I'll be fine.

JED. And I know you feel the same way about Mom, about a lot of things back there. You know what I mean?

(no response)

Just think about it.

*(**KYLIE** gets up and moves towards the door.)*

Where are you going?

KYLIE. On a walk…to think about it.

*(**KYLIE** exits, **JED** picks up the guitar and strums quietly.)*

Scene Sixteen

*(**GUNTHER** is sitting on the side of a road with his backpack and stuffed octopus and wearing **KYLIE**'s wings. He has a map and sandwich out and is trying to puzzle out the map.)*

GUNTHER. North is…

(He stretches his arm out with his index finger pointed and swings the arm around with his eyes closed.)

that way?

(He opens his eyes and sees his finger is pointed upwards. He sighs.)

Great! *(He shouts into the sky.)* Are you up there Kyrie? I didn't think so. Oh well, I took my oath as a superhero that one must not leave the others to die.

(He looks at the map again and then turns to his stuffed octopus.)

Cheetah, I didn't raise you from the dead and get the Pirate and Slave Trading Company to agree not to chase us for no reason. You have to help me!

(He rests his elbows on his knees and his head on his hands and pouts.)

We're lost.

(pause)

How could I get lost in my own galaxy? I told you when she left that the Superhero Destruction Industry would find her, but she didn't even come and ask for my advice.

(He sighs again and then looks at the map.)

Well, we've been on this whole side, *(he traces his finger around a portion of the map)* so the only other option Cheetah, is that she crossed to the other side, and there's the river we have to cross. I know, it's full of acid, but Cheetah, we have to get Kyrie! Kyrie said that it's just water…so maybe it won't hurt.

(He pauses.)

GUNTHER. *(cont.)* It is kinda big. What if I can't touch the bottom?

(He pauses again and then looks at the stuffed octopus.)

You're right. I have to get Kyrie. She would do it for me, and I know she's over there. It's only water…right?

Scene Seventeen

*(**KYLIE** and her **MOM** enter the living room. They're both carrying bags and enter talking)*

KYLIE. We played in the park, just songs we both knew, and then people started putting money in our guitar cases, which was kind of cool. But then Jed started dancing and it was tragic.

MOTHER. That's great. Sounds like Jed's happy. Oh, Kylie, you know that kid you babysat?

KYLIE. Gunther?

MOTHER. Yeah, something like that. He came by and left this for you.

(She goes to the table and grabs an action figure and passes it to KYLIE.)

He said it was for something you were building?

KYLIE. My mobile. Right. I didn't think he was listening…

MOTHER. Your what?

KYLIE. I'll have to show you later.

MOTHER. Ok.

KYLIE. After dinner maybe?

MOTHER. I was thinking we could make something together. Spaghetti maybe?

KYLIE. Sure. Oh, before I forget,

(She digs through her bag and then presents her mom with a cd.)

This is for you. Jed and I made it. It's songs from some of his live concerts.

MOTHER. Thank you. I –

KYLIE. *(referencing the bags)* I should take these to my room.

MOTHER. All right. Kylie?

KYLIE. Yeah?

MOTHER. I'm glad you're back.

*(**KYLIE** smiles and exits with bags and action figure.)*

Scene Eighteen

*(**GUNTHER** is on a hospital bed and **KYLIE** is on a chair beside him. **GUNTHER** looks like he is just waking up.)*

KYLIE. How are you feeling Gunther?

GUNTHER. Kyrie!!!!

KYLIE. Better apparently.

GUNTHER. *(in a hurry to explain it all)* You left, Kyrie. I didn't know where you went! I finally decided that you must have gotten lost. I took a map with me and tried to find you, but you weren't anywhere. I even raised Cheetah from the dead so that he could help me find you. The Pirate and Slave Trading Company even agreed not to chase us after a while so that we could look for you.

KYLIE. Did they really?

GUNTHER. Uh-huh. And we searched and searched. I ended up having to eat both my sandwiches and yours. Sorry, Kyrie.

KYLIE. That's all right Gunther. I'm glad you're feeling better, that's all. But do you realize how stupid you were?

GUNTHER. It was just a river. You said that water couldn't hurt me. I checked all over this side. I thought that you'd probably be on the other side. I had to cross it.

KYLIE. You almost drowned.

GUNTHER. You told me water couldn't hurt me.

KYLIE. It wasn't the water that hurt you Gunther, it was the current.

GUNTHER. What's that?

KYLIE. One day I promise I will teach you all about the physics of currents, but I can ALSO promise you that it won't be today.

GUNTHER. At least I'm not scared of water any more. That's a good thing, right?

KYLIE. I'm not so sure. Do me a favor.

GUNTHER. What?

KYLIE. Don't go jumping in any more rivers, or streams, or lakes, or pools, or even bath tubs unless your mom, your grandma, or I am watching and tell you it's ok.

GUNTHER. I already promised mom and Miss Nanny that.

KYLIE. Just promise me too.

GUNTHER. Ok, I promise.

KYLIE. And another thing…

GUNTHER. What?

KYLIE. Don't go chasing me.

GUNTHER. But Kyrie, you were gone for so long. I didn't think that you were coming back.

KYLIE. Promise.

GUNTHER. I promise. I promise. I promise. I promise. I promise. I promise. I promise.

KYLIE. Thanks Gunther. Guess what?

GUNTHER. *(gloomily)* You're going to kill me if I go after you again?

KYLIE. That too. But I decided I don't like the cities.

GUNTHER. Why not?

KYLIE. Because our town has something that they don't.

GUNTHER. What?

KYLIE. Gunthers. And I don't think that I could live without those anymore.

GUNTHER. Any superheroes there?

KYLIE. Nope.

GUNTHER. Must be pretty boring. *(pause)* Kyrie! Now it's your turn to guess.

KYLIE. We have to have another funeral for Cheetah?

GUNTHER. No. Well, we should. But it's different. I made three shots in the basketball hoop and life doesn't suck anymore!

KYLIE. Good job! When you get better are you gonna teach me to play basketball?

GUNTHER. Yep. You gonna teach me to swim?

KYLIE. Yep.

GUNTHER. Right then.

End Of Play

A FUNERAL FOR MITTENS

67

by Samuel French

CHARACTERS

Dan

Carolyn

Max

ABOUT THE PLAYWRIGHT

Samuel French has attended arts schools since kindergarden and has been writing for as long as he can remember. His one-act *Writer's Block* was the first-place winner of the 2008 Baker's Plays High School Playwriting Competition and was subsequently published the first volume of Dramatic Debuts, available from Baker's Plays. Sam will study playwriting and directing in college.

(DAN [17] sits watching T.V. He scratches his balls. He changes the channel to an episode of "Everybody Loves Raymond." He laughs to himself.)

DAN. Ha. Raymond.

(He refers to his phone, reading some unknown text. The text is amusing to him, but his balls still itch. He contemplates for a minute which is more urgent, the text or his balls. The balls win out. The mood is relaxed. The mood is shattered by the entrance of CAROLYN [16], followed by her boyfriend, MAX [17]. CAROLYN is distraught, as usual. MAX is following CAROLYN, as usual. DAN, chill as usual, watches the following scene unfold with the same disinterested disposition that the possessed while attending to his itchy balls.)

CAROLYN. Oh my God. Oh my God. Oh my God. I'm going to hell.

MAX. You're not!

CAROLYN. I am!

MAX. No! You're not!

CAROLYN. I'm gonna be with like…Hitler, and Ted Bundy, and those people in Sweden who club baby seals!

MAX. No, you won't be!

CAROLYN. Yes, I will…be! I will be in hell with the murderers and the rapists and the people who club baby seals on the heads with ice picks!

MAX. Will you help me? Jesus.

DAN. What? Help you with what?

MAX. She thinks she hit a dog.

DAN. Oh, holy shit! You hit a dog!?!?!

MAX. No! She *thinks* she hit a dog. She could be mistaken. Like. Like, it could have been a tree branch. Like, lying in the middle of the road.

CAROLYN. It woofed!

MAX. Like, lying in the middle of the road in a way that it could have scraped against your car and made a woofy noise. Sticks do that all the time…Yeah. Right, Dan? Don't sticks scraping against cars sometimes go woof?

DAN. No. They never do. They might go "screeechhhhh," or "chhhhh." But woof? *Dogs* go woof.

*(***CAROLYN*** sobs.)*

MAX. Screw you.

DAN. Hey!

MAX. Carolyn. It was dark. You couldn't see. Your mind's just exaggerating. You probably hit a branch. Or a piece of a tire. Or, like, –

DAN. A child.

(She sobs harder.)

A young child.

MAX. Dude! What the hell!?!

DAN. I'm just trying to help.

MAX. HOW!? HOW COULD THAT HELP!?!

DAN. Well…'cause then like…then she didn't hit a dog.

MAX. Honey. You didn't hit a child. It went woof, remember? Children don't go woof!

DAN. Unless they were just learning to speak. You know, "what noise does the monkey make?" "Ooeeoooaa!" "What noise does the sheep make?" "Baaaaa!" "What noise does the doggy make?""Woof!" BAM! CRASH…. In that case, a child would say woof.

MAX. ALRIGHT. WHAT THE HELL IS WRONG WITH YOU?

DAN. Hey! Let he who is without sin cast the first stone.

*(Beat. **MAX** is aghast.)*

MAX. WHAT?!

DAN. I'm just saying no one's perfect.

MAX. MY GIRLFRIEND, YOUR FRIEND, IS DISTRAUGHT. DISTRAUGHT 'CAUSE SHE JUST HIT A DOG – or a tree branch – WITH HER CAR AND YOUR CONSOLATION IS TELLING HER "DON'T WORRY, IT MIGHT NOT HAVE BEEN A DOG, IT MIGHT JUST HAVE BEEN A HUMAN CHILD." HOLY SHIT! *JESUS* WOULD STONE YOU FOR THAT.

DAN. He would not.

MAX. Yeah. He would.

DAN. Well, he was without sin, so he'd be allowed to.

MAX. I'm just saying…Calm down and be okay for once. Right? She's upset. I know it's funny 'cause like she loves animals, but calm the hell down and be her friend.

DAN. I'm sorry, Carolyn. You're not going to hell. You didn't hit a dog, and even if you did, hell is too full of the murderers and baby seal ice pickers to fit you in.

(*Long pause.* **CAROLYN** *just sniffles.*)

CAROLYN. …what if it had mittens?

MAX. Huh?

CAROLYN. Like mittens…Like a black dog with white paws. Mittens. Mittens are adorable. What if it had mittens? If it had mittens I wouldn't be able to live with myself.

MAX. It wasn't a dog, so it didn't have mittens.

CAROLYN. My dog had mittens. Zeus had mittens. That's why we named him Zeus.

(*Beat. No one understands.*)

DAN. What the he –

MAX. Carolyn. That makes no sense.

CAROLYN. Well, it's like with the…. And the mitte…and… yeah.

MAX. No. Carolyn. It doesn't make sense.

CAROLYN. Ok. I just thought… And you're supposed to always agree with me! You're supposed to support me! When I need you! And I need you now! 'Cause I killed an adorable dog with mittens and his owners hate me and God hates me and you haaaaate me, too.

(**MAX** *is tired of this shit.*)

MAX. Oh, come on. Give me a break! I'm trying to be supportive. But I don't understand what the big deal is!

DAN. Dude!!

MAX. No! Come on. Calm the hell down. So you hit a dog, and killed it, and it's dead.

(**CAROLYN** *sobs.*)

Yeah. That's the truth. I hate seeing you upset! I really do! And I want to make you happy! But I have a hard time doing that when I don't understand what's really wrong! I like dogs as much as the next guy. You know. They're cute. They wag their tails and chase balls. But it's not the end of the world that you've hit one.

CAROLYN. You don't understand! I'm not a killer! I love gardens. And animals. And hemp merchandise! And maybe the thought of taking the life of one of God's creatures appeals to you, but not to me! And I look at my hands right now and all I can see is blood. There's blood on my hands. CAN'T YOU SEE THE BLOOD ON MY HANDS?

MAX. Okay, now. That's a bit over-dramatic, isn't it?

(**CAROLYN** *storms out of the room.* **DAN** *follows her with his eyes in amazement. As she leaves, he turns to* **MAX**, *who has sunk down to the couch in defeat.*)

DAN. Okay. First off…

MAX. Shut up, man.

DAN. No. No. Like *seriously…*

MAX. I said shut up.

(**MAX** *covers his face with a pillow and screams his frustration into it.*)

AAAGGGGGGGGGGGGGGGGGGGGHHHHHHHHHHH-HHHHHHH!!!!!!!!!

(**DAN** *is uncomfortable. Like the turtle, he retreats from dangerous situations and distances himself from* **MAX**.*)

MAX. *(cont.)* What can I do, Dan? I'm trying to be compassionate and sympathetic and all that crap, but I really don't get it. I love her. I do. But I can't begin to understand why this is such a big deal. To me, it was an accident. So what's the big deal? I don't get it.

DAN. Well. Sometimes you've gotta fake it. Pretend you care about a problem your friend is having when actually you couldn't care less.

MAX. Man, it's not that easy.

DAN. No. It is that easy. I do it all the time.

*(**MAX** stares **DAN** down, counting in his mind the numerous times **DAN** must have faked caring for him.)*

MAX. That time when I found out I was failing geom –

DAN. Yep.

MAX. What about that time when Carolyn's mom told me tha –

DAN. Yep.

MAX. And when my grandmother passed?

DAN. Yep.

MAX. So. It's all been fake?!

DAN. What did you expect? Don't get all moody. I made you feel better. That's what mattered.

MAX. Fine…Am I good to her?

DAN. I dunno. She's bawling in my bathroom and you're sitting here talking to me.

MAX. Okay. Right. Fake it. Thanks?

*(**DAN** retires to the couch as **MAX** walks up and calls out to **CAROLYN**.)*

CAROLYN? HONEY?

(All that is heard is a gibberish howl of dismay.)

You gotta come out now. I was a little harsh before, but, like, I was just trying to say that maybe it is time to face reality. So you probably did hit a dog, and I'm guessing it's probably not okay. But that's okay.

MAX. *(cont.)* It might hurt you, and some other people, but in the end I know you're going to still be a good person, and you're going to be strong and take responsibility for this accident. Because you are a strong, good person.

(The wailing slowly fades. Silence. **DAN** *is watching.)*

So you gotta come out and think about what we're going to do. I don't know exactly what we should d…. but we could contact the neighbors, or go look with flashlights, or…

*(***CAROLYN*** *reenters.)*

CAROLYN. I think we should give Mittens the dog a funeral.

DAN. Er. Shall it be open casket?

CAROLYN. You're an idiot. And I'm serious. That's the only way I can get some closure. I need to give the dog a funeral.

MAX. Alright. Of course. How can we help?

CAROLYN. Dan. Can you find me like…a shoe box…and ties for you and Max. You both look like crap. This is formal.

DAN. Er. Yeah. Right. Hold on…

*(***DAN*** *exits.)*

MAX. Look. I'm sorry I said all that. I was overwhelmed and didn't know how to react.

CAROLYN. I get it. It's fine. Let's bury this dog…metaphorically.

MAX. Okay. So crisis averted?

*(***CAROLYN*** *laughs.)*

CAROLYN. Crisis averted…Like yeah, that's a little gay "Crisis Averted, Captain." A bit gay but okay, sure, Max. Crisis averted.

(She kisses him. He is no longer embarrassed. **DAN** *enters, carrying a shoe box, wearing a tie and a blazer; he is making an effort. He brought a bow tie for* **MAX***; he still has his sense of humor.)*

MAX. Are you kidding me? Fine. So how do we do this?

> (**CAROLYN** *places the shoe box on the ground. They form a semicircle around it,* **CAROLYN** *in the middle.* **MAX** *and* **DAN** *stand awkwardly, not knowing what to do.* **CAROLYN**, *on the other hand, is in the moment. She stares at the box, clenching her fists, her eyes bright with precursors to tears. Her voice is shaky.*)

> (*Throughout* **CAROLYN**'s *following monologue, the boys communicate to each other behind her back with various facial expressions, representing confusion, bewilderment, and more. They also are constantly trying to stifle their laughter.*)

CAROLYN. Poor Mittens, I didn't know you very well. I would have liked to. I feel, however, that I can speak as if I did know you…You were a great dog. Majestic and proud. Small, but scrappy. You sniffed at every tree, howled at every mailman, You woofed, you ran, you slobbered. You lived your life like a candle in the wind, never fading with the sunset when the rain set in…I don't know why God chose to end your life so soon, I don't know why God chose to make you crossing the street exactly at the moment. I don't know why the Toyota manufacturers chose to design the front of my Prius to be so damn durable. But they did. And that was all it took. 5 star safety rating, right smack in your face. Assholes…I like to think you died happy, chasing after some symbolic dream. I like to think that you had lived a good, long life. A good, 6 year long life. A good….er….42 year long in dog years life. I like to think that. And I know I will miss having never known you. And I know, most of all, that your owners will miss you. You spent your life digging up holes in their backyard, and have now dug one last final hole…in all of our hearts…Guys. Would you like to say something?

MAX. Oh. Right. Er. I like to think that you don't know what happened, and you're still chasing our car, all the way to heaven.

CAROLYN. That was chillingly beautiful. Dan?

DAN. I'm not really good at this sort of thing.

CAROLYN. Dan.

DAN. Er. "Once more unto the breach."

CAROLYN. Amen.

DAN. Amen.

MAX. Amen.

> *(They look at each other.* **DAN** *and* **MAX** *still in an awkward shock.* **CAROLYN** *now able to appreciate the ridiculousness of the matter. The phone rings.)*

DAN. Hold on.

> *(He exits.* **MAX** *and* **CAROLYN** *stare at each other. She laughs and kisses him.)*

CAROLYN. Thank you.

MAX. You know. You really shouldn't blame yourself. It was out of your hands.

CAROLYN. I know. Even so, I can't help but hate myself a little. I mean. I don't blame myself for hitting the dog, but I hate myself. I don't blame Dan for being an asshole, but I still hate him.

MAX. You don't really hate yourself, do you?

> *(***DAN*** *walks in, talking on the phone.)*

DAN. I'm so sorry, Mrs. Wainwright. We were about to go door to door asking…I'm really sorry…Okay…Of course.
I understand…Well…Okay…Thank you so much. We're so sorry.

CAROLYN. Ask her if it had mittens!

DAN. Oh. Um. Did Moose happen to have mittens?…You know, mittens. Like when a black dog has white paws… Yeah. Mittens…Yes. They are adorable…

> *(to* **CAROLYN***)*

No, it didn't have mittens. Moose was all brown.

CAROLYN. Ask her if I could come over and talk to her for a few…

DAN. Would you mind if she came over for a few minutes? She'd really like to ask you some questions…Thank you very much…And again, we're so sorry. Thanks. Bye.

*(**DAN** hangs up and sighs.)*

Moose. What a dumbass name.

CAROLYN. Max. I'm going to…I'll be back soon.

*(She exits out the front door. **MAX** and **DAN** remain alone. **MAX** breathes a sigh of relief.)*

MAX. You're right. Moose is a dumb name.

(beat)

So all this caring. It's all fake? All an act?

DAN. Right.

MAX. Well, that's tough. I've gotta work on that.

DAN. The important thing is that you *want* to understand and care.

MAX. Right. That's the important thing. Not that you actually *don't* car –

DAN. – don't care. No. That's not important. You can fake that.

MAX. Yeah. I've gotta work on that.

DAN. Well, practice makes perfect.

MAX. You're pretty damn good.

DAN. I get a lot of practice.

MAX. Pretty damn good…Wanna watch some Raymond?

(lights fade)

MAKING BABIES

79

by Paxton Grey Farrar

ORIGINAL PRODUCTION CAST

PONS . . . . .Ella Mora

TIBIA . . . . .Amy Helmuth

ABDOMINIS . . . . Nick Goodman

FEMORAL . . . . .Jesse Stout

HAMSTRING. . . . . .Charlie McDonell

TOUCH . . . . .Maddie Davis

CEREBELLUM . . . . Clinton Bradford

PATELLA-UTERUS. . . . . .Madie Polyak

SANDY . . . . Anna Jansen

LEONARDO . . . . Jon Lee

CAMEO . . . . .Bryan Marenstein

Produced by . . . . Ruben Van Kempen, Elizabeth Orme, Gregory Malins

CHARACTERS

PONS – Project lead, facilitator. (M/F)

TOUCH – Annoying, hyper teenager, nobody pays attention to. (F)

FEMORAL – Cultured, gay, artistic, neat, sensitive. (M)

HAMSTRING – Jock, healthy, good-build, conservative. (M)

TIBIA – Attractive, concerned with appearance, into the opposite sex.
(F)

CEREBELLUM – Nerd, intelligent, obsessive-compulsive. (M/F)

ABDOMINIS – Slob, lazy, with a sarcastic sense of humor. (M)

PATELLA-UTERUS: Politically correct, lecturing-teacher-type. (F)

SANDY – Calmly reading a romance novel, seen it all before, quiet until
Part 3. (M/F)

LEONARDO – Skateboarder, dreadlocks, got it together, Character of
Part 3. (M/F)

ABOUT THE PLAYWRIGHT

At time of writing, Paxton Farrar is a senior at Roosevelt High School in
Seattle, Washington. He wrote and directed *Making Babies*, his first play,
in the 2008 Roosevelt Drama Festival of Student Directed One-Act Plays.
For his Senior Project, he produced the first act of his original musi-
cal for which he wrote the book, music, lyrics, score and performed as
musical director. It was showcased at the 2009 Roosevelt Drama Festival.
Currently, he is working on a children's book. He plans on moving to
New York City in the fall of 2010.

PART 1:
The team works to construct the gene sequence of a human.

(All is dark; a large spotlight comes up in the middle of the stage illuminating a table ringed by nine office chairs. Figures dressed as sperm swirl around a round table to bubbly/squishy/muffled noises. Many make feinted attempts at the chairs. Slowly one cautiously, but purposely, approaches the table, pulls out a chair and flops onto the table. Light on the table goes out. Exit sperm. Swirl of pastel colored blobs of light all over the stage. Orchestral music starts [e.g. Richard Strauss' "Also Sprach Zarathustra"].)

(blackout)

(Lights come up on long table with a clear center position for a moderator. The table may be angled like a shallow "V" or as a horseshoe or straight across like a panel. Nine figures are present in a typical office meeting environment: a coffee station to one side, etc. [In the original production, as a sight-gag, the 9 figures were posed in a representation of The Last Supper *by Leonardo da Vinci – only long enough for the audience to figure it out and then the actors broke and took their seats.])*

PONS. Ok, so let's get this project meeting started. I need to take roll: *(Calls the following names and they answer as below:)*

TIBIA. Here.

ABDOMINIS. Yah.

FEMORAL. Present.

HAMSTRING. Here.

TOUCH. *(not seated – roaming the room)* You can see me. I am right here.

CEREBELLUM. Check.

PATELLA-UTERUS. Present and accounted for.

PONS. Have I missed anyone?

SANDY. *(looks up from her book)* Sandy's here.

PONS. Oh, yes, of course…and Sandy.

PONS. Glad you all could make it, I know you've had a *rousing* trip but we're all here now and we have a lot to do in a short space of time.

ABDOMINIS. What time is it anyway?

PONS. Well, the TV went off about five minutes ago.

TIBIA. *(quietly to the one next to her)* Five minutes – good grief; hardly worth it.

PONS. *(scowling at* **TIBIA,** *and then moving on)* Just to make the project timeline clear, the meeting has started with your arrival and we have about two seconds to complete the helix before the cell splits. So I suggest we get on it – but before we do I have something I wanted to lay out on the table. It's what we've all been thinking. We messed up last time – messed up bad. Have you seen the parents? It's a testament to Darwin that we are here today. But we are here. And the important thing is that we do it right this time. Now before we get started are there any questions?

ABDOMINIS. *(listless)* Are you sure we are doing this? This isn't a false alarm?

PONS. Oh, no. We are definitely pregnant.

FEMORAL. Well she's going to be surprised later this month.

PATELLA-UTERUS. *(lecturing)* She shouldn't be. She knows very well what she's been doing.

CEREBELLUM. Him?

TOUCH. *(looks up)* Bow Chicka Bow Wow *(High hat moment)*

(She then attempts a fist bump with **CEREBELLUM** *who messes it up by awkwardly shaking her fist.)*

PATELLA-UTERUS. *(still lecturing)* Yes! There are consequences for one's actions.

PONS. *(exaggerated and preacher-like)* And what glorious and wonderful consequences we have here today. Pregnancy! So if there are no further questions, let us begin.

TIBIA. I think we should start with the eyes – pretty eyes.

HAMSTRING. Hold on, hold on, I remember the last time we started with eyes. We ended up with a pretty package, but it was four foot nine. We have to start with skeletal structure – and I recommend six six.

CEREBELLUM. No. No. No. You lose ten points of IQ for every inch over six feet. That would give the project – *(starts tapping a calculator)*

ABDOMINIS. Retarded. The damn thing would be retarded.

PATELLA-UTERUS. Silence you idiot. You can't say retarded anymore. You must say mentally challeng – –

CEREBELLUM. *(finishes tapping the calculator and looks up as if nothing else had transpired)* …the IQ of a duck.

HAMSTRING. Ok, but height has been linked to success in our past projects. So I still say –

TOUCH. I have a suggestion. Why don't we compromise?

FEMORAL. *(completely ignoring **TOUCH**)* Skinny. I like skinny.

TOUCH. *(still searching for an audience)* We could compromise?

TIBIA. *(insistent)* Eyes guys.

TOUCH. *(desperate for attention)* We could compromise?

CEREBELLUM. IQ. IQ. IQ. Smarts is everything.

TOUCH. *(looking around to see if anybody is listening)* We could compromise?

PONS. *(completely ignoring **TOUCH**)* I have an idea, let's compromise. As I always say – it's all about compromise. *(turns to **CEREBELLUM**)* Shorten it up enough to have the IQ of…an actor.

(long silence)

Ok…let's do it.

(**PONS** *pulls out large unwieldy papers. Murmur begins, lights fade out/fade in. It should appear that some time has passed.*)

PONS. *(cont.)* Ok so we've got the frame and the internal organs, this is good people, we're making progress. And we still have a second to go.

TIBIA. I still say we're getting ahead of everything. We need to first talk about hair color. If we pick the right hair color everything else will fall into place. If it's a blond we won't even need to worry about the brain.

FEMORAL. Well I say dark everything. Let's have a mocha java, no foam latte.

HAMSTRING. Nope. We only have two-pump vanilla to work with. Didn't you get that memo? It was in the functional spec. Both the parents are snowflakes. But we could still have a Quarterback. We haven't had a Quarterback type in years. That's just what we need to insure maximum project success in today's world.

TOUCH. *(looking over the prints from afar and commenting quietly)* What a nose.

TIBIA. *(ignoring **TOUCH** but absentmindedly grabbing the blue print)* We have to do something about this nose.

PATELLA-UTERUS. *(indignant)* What's wrong with it?

ABDOMINIS. *(sarcastic)* What's wrong with it? It'll have to be named Cyrano.

PONS. *(begins pulling cards/pages/props showing noses)* How bout this?…How bout this?…How bout this?…

TIBIA. *(answering **PONS**)* No…No…No…Well that one is kinda interesting.

CEREBELLUM. It's kind of big, isn't it?

ABDOMINIS. *(raising his eyebrows)* Well, you know what that means. We will have to give him a big dihh –

PATELLA-UTERUS. *(interrupting, jumping up, inflamed, loud)* Don't use that word. How can you say that? Who do you think you are, you sexist pig? *(yelling)* You cannot say *HIM*. That has not been decided yet. Pons, get control of this thing.

PONS. *(tapping for attention)* Out of Order. Out of Order. Patella-Uterus is correct, Abdominis. You must say IT – or PROJECT, until the gender is decided and we are not there yet.

FEMORAL. *(jumping in late, but eager)* Can he be gay?

ABDOMINIS. Oh, god. You do this every time…

(The whole table erupts in opinions and a general pandemonium.)

PATELLA-UTERUS. *(yelling over everyone)* PONS!

*(***PONS*** makes a gesture that cuts everyone off, except **ABDOMINIS** who wants to finish his sentence.)*

ABDOMINIS. …visible from every angle.

PONS. *(tapping for attention)* Out of Order. Out of Order. Femoral, pay attention. We have not decided –

FEMORAL. *(interrupting)* Can he at least be neat?

PONS. Femoral, you are not listening. The gender has not been –

FEMORAL. *(still not getting it)* Can she be a lesbian?

PONS. *(getting agitated)* Damn it, Femoral. It is not a she *or* a he. The gender has not been decided, much less the sexual orientation. Do you understand?

FEMORAL. *(resolved)* Yes, I get it… Questioning youth… *(with an aside)* IT could start a club.

HAMSTRING. Ok then, well IT hasn't been decided. But if we go with that nose and IT is not a HIM, then SHE will have big… *(looking around for a word)* Mam-mam… Mammarr… Mammalianeeee

CEREBELLUM. *(offering)* Boobs?

HAMSTRING. Yes. Big boobs.

GROUP. *(roundly agreeing)* Yes. Of course. What else, etc.…

PART 2:
Team begins to slowly fall apart and go at each other.

PONS. Have we decided on this nose then?

TIBIA. *(wavering)* Well, maybe. The nose must fit the face. IT needs to be good looking. Ugly people have to work too hard. Look at all the celebrities. They don't do a thing – they just party.

CEREBELLUM. That is because they are rich.

TIBIA. That is how you GET rich, Cerebellum. By being beautiful – it's a sure ticket to the millionaires' club.

PONS. It is not our responsibility here to incur social or economic status.

PATELLA-UTERUS. Oh, give me a break. What we do here in the next *(looks at her watch)* half-second will decide 100% of ITS social status. Beautiful people, aggressive people, sometimes even talented people – they all live higher in the pecking order. Smart people only have a 20% chance, but that is better than zero. And zero is what dumb and ugly gets you. Maybe not a pretty truth, but truth all the same.

ABDOMINIS. *(sarcastic)* Patella-Uterus, you have such a rosy, positive view.

PATELLA-UTERUS. Be quiet, you missing chromosome.

ABDOMINIS. *(defensive)* Oh. Bring that up again. I go missing, *once* – on one project – and you treat me like ... like...a village idiot. *(defensive)* Well IT became president. *(He takes out and lights up a cigar.)*

FEMORAL. *(jumping up)* Hey! This is a smoke-free uterus.

ABDOMINIS. *(putting it out)* Ah, get lost.

PONS. *(looking for something)* Speaking of lost, has anyone seen the other box.

GROUP. No, not here...etc.

PONS. Well it should have already been here. Touch, would you look under there... *(opening the box on hand)* Well, here is the X as you would expect.

(**PONS** *pulls a giant X out of the box.*)

PONS. *(cont.)* Well, this is quite proper. But not having the other box is quite irregular.

(There is a rumble and squeak of brakes like a delivery truck. You hear the back door roll up and down. **CAMEO** *walks onto the stage dressed in a delivery uniform and carrying a cardboard box.)*

CAMEO. Special Delivery.

PONS. About time. You are very late. Where is your pink –

CAMEO. *(handing him a typical high school pinkslip)* Apologies sir. Here will you please sign?

PONS. Sure. *(taking a pen from* **CAMEO** *who pulls it from behind his ear)* Charge it to the father.

CAMEO. *(on exit)* No charge sir. On time delivery was guaranteed.

PONS. *(handing it to* **FEMORAL**) Will you do the honors?

FEMORAL. *(Opens the box delicately with switchblade handed to him by* **TOUCH**. *He looks in and smiles and then pulls out another big X.)* IT's a girl!

(The **WOMEN** *and* **FEMORAL** *jump up and high five, etc except* **TIBIA** *who drops her face into cradled hands. No one pays any attention until it calms down and* **PONS** *takes notice.)*

HAMSTRING. Damn it! That happens like half the time. It's ridiculous!

PONS. TIBIA, what's wrong, I thought you –

TIBIA. *(exasperated)* What's wrong!? I tell you what's wrong. She's wearing size 10 feet.

(All the **WOMEN** *collapse into their seats, devastated.)*

HAMSTRING. Well those are great if she wants to be a quarterback.

CEREBELLUM. *(helpful)* She could be a swimmer.

TOUCH. *(put out)* Shut Up, Cerebellum.

TIBIA. *(whining)* I knew we shoulda waited on the gender-box before deciding on the feet. We let Hamstring pressure us into it. And now we have a closet full of ugly shoes.

(Beat. She goes quiet and then asks:)

Could we trade?

FEMORAL. *(resigned)* There's not much left to trade.

TOUCH. We could give up some more IQ points. Small feet; big boobs – who needs smarts.

PATELLA-UTERUS. OH, Grow up.

TOUCH. I am 800 Million years old.

PATELLA-UTERUS. When you have a billion years, come and talk to me. You are so immature.

TOUCH. Well at least I'm not an old troglodyte like you. Look at you – you still wear a wristwatch. I have an iPhone *[or current technology]*.

(pulls out her iPhone and starts playing with it)

You want me to call for a wheelchair. Or how bout I play some *sixties* music for you.

(An iconic 1960s song blares for a moment.)*

CEREBELLUM. *(after music stops)* I like that song.

ABDOMINIS. *(joining the heckle)* Yeah, you tell her girl.

TOUCH. You're just as bad. Look at you: you're wearing overalls, you're fat, you smoke –

ABDOMINIS. Hey, maybe if you showed a little respect you'd get some back.

CEREBELLUM. Now look, her rebellious attitude is an important part of the human social structure, necessary to the creation of a new generation of leaders.

HAMSTRING. I am getting really tired of your facts and figures four-eyes. Human beings need to be made with passion and determination. Not numbers and theories.

---

*Please see Music Use Note on Page 3.

TIBIA. You dumb jocks are all alike.

FEMORAL. *(standing and grabbing his things)* People, people! I can't work with this! Call me when you can handle yourselves with manners and dignity. I am going outside.

ABDOMINIS. *(also standing and grabbing his cigar)* That's the best idea I've heard all day. I'm gonna go outside and have a smoke.

PATELLA-UTERUS. *(gathering her things)* I think I'll be off too. It's always everyone against me so I'll just make it easier on all of us.

(**CEREBELLUM** *has been quietly and neatly packing his briefcase and avoiding making eye-contact.* **PONS** *is desperately trying to keep the meeting together.* **TOUCH** *has been buried in her phone and jittering, occasionally looking around.* **FEMORAL, ABDOMINIS,** *and* **PATELLA-UTERUS** *are gathering their things and moving slowly to the sides.* **SANDY** *has been calmly reading.* **TIBIA** *and* **HAMSTRING** *now alone at the table, look around and then stare across at each other.)*

HAMSTRING. You know I always thought you were a waste of amino acids. All you ever want is a pretty project. Your's is a world where people just breed like rabbits and never achieve anything!

TIBIA. *(She stands and moves closer to* **HAMSTRING.***)* All you want is a world without feelings and relationships, where everyone is macho and ripped and they all play football!

HAMSTRING. *(He stands and closes half the distance.)* Harlot!

TIBIA. *(She closes half the distance.)* Meat head!

HAMSTRING. *(He closes half the distance.* **TIBIA** *and he are now face to face.)* Slut!

TIBIA. Dick!

HAMSTRING. You make me so hot!

TIBIA. I know.

(**TIBIA** *and* **HAMSTRING** *grab each other. Make-out scene. They fall to the ground where they begin to roll around in an outrageous display. The others stop and stare for a moment, then move on.* **SANDY** *looks over, mildly interested, then back to her book.* **TOUCH** *clumsily grabs the blueprints/models/books and attempts to run away with them.* **PONS** *chases and stops her.*)

PART 3:
A newcomer unites the team against him and then unites the team with him.

*(Sounds of a skateboard coming down a sidewalk, click-ity clack. The actors freeze, listening. A guy in dreadlocks comes coasting onto the stage, pops his skateboard up to catch it and takes a seat near **SANDY**, who is still calmly reading. The others stop what they are doing and start to congregate in a group opposite the newcomer.)*

TOUCH. Who are you?

LEONARDO. I've come to join your project.

PONS. *(back in the moderator spot, rustles through some paper-work)* I don't see you on the roster.

PATELLA-UTERUS. You look very suspicious.

FEMORAL. You look very familiar. What is your name?

LEONARDO. *(speaking quietly)* Leonardo.

ABDOMINIS. What did you say?

LEONARDO. *(speaking louder)* Leonardo.

ABDOMINIS. *(pontificating)* What kinda name is that? Leonardo. Who the hell are you?

TOUCH. *(realizing what he is and jumping up in excitement)* You're a Mutant. That's what you are. A Mutant. Right here on our project – a mutant. Oh-my-god this is amaaaazing.

*(The table erupts. Lots of comments. Lots of gesturing, denials, etc. **LEONARDO** takes it all in stride. When they sit down they are on one side of the table and **LEONARDO** is isolated on his side with **SANDY**.)*

PONS. *(flustered)* Well this is all most unusual. It has been so long. I am not sure of the procedure. (**PONS** *begins consulting his paperwork.)*

TOUCH. *(gushing as if she is talking to a rock-star)* Whoaaaah. You're really interesting. Are you a good mutant or … *(with relish and anticipation)* a baaaaaad mutant?

LEONARDO. *(quiet, confident and serene)* Depends. It always depends on your point of view?

ABDOMINIS. *(agitated)* Well my point of view is that all mutants are bad. And you look like a right-bad one. It's genes like you what give us good genes a bad name.

PATELLA-UTERUS. *(getting closer to* **ABDOMINIS***)* I agree with you, ABDOMINIS.

CEREBELLUM. *(looking through a huge book and reading from it)* Most mutations are rather neutral but some can cause vast changes in the chromosomes. The re-sequencing can cause major evolutionary shifts. It is how elephants got their trunks and horny toads got their…Well you know…their horny.

TIBIA. *(getting interested)* Well what if Leonardo brought something exciting to the project. Like a sixth sense. Like being able to know *what* boys are thinking.

HAMSTRING. Or super strength, maybe revolutionary vision and superb throwing accuracy… *(fakes a football throw)*

PATELLA-UTERUS. *(finishing the sentence)* A leader of men.

FEMORAL. *(warming up to it)* Or artistic brilliance. She could be a great artist like…Donatello.

TOUCH. *(warming up to it)* Or Rafael.

TIBIA. *(warming up to it)* Or Michelangelo.

   (beat)

CEREBELLUM. *(awkward and out of step with the cadence)* True mathematic understanding?

ABDOMINIS. *(sarcastic)* Well I think he is a bad mutation. You look unhealthy boy. Your eyes are all bloodshot.

LEONARDO. I was up late. Studying. *(to* **FEMORAL***)* Are you gonna eat those chips?

   *(***FEMORAL** *tosses a bag to him.)*

CEREBELLUM. *(reading from the large book)* Some of the worst mistakes of evolution have come from mutations. On the other hand, some of life's greatest achievements have come from mutations.

PONS. *(now also looking at the large book over* **CEREBELLUM**'s *shoulder)* It's a high stakes crap shoot. What do you guys think?

ABDOMINIS. Why risk it? We have an excellent project as it is.

TIBIA. What if she ends up with some abnormality because of him – like bad hair? Project end! No more little projects.

PATELLA-UTERUS. She could be socially inept. Or a bad student.

CEREBELLUM. The odds do not favor his admission. So many things could go wrong.

PONS. *(reading from another book)* The procedure is thus: The dominant genes, as represented by the Expected Chromosomes – that would be us – can crowd out the mutant if they work as a team. The Expected Chromosomes must reach a unanimous vote to accept, or block, the mutant from the helix – before the mutant can insert itself.

PATELLA-UTERUS. If all you idiots hadn't been fighting about boobs, we would have finished before he got here – and there wouldn't be any question of letting him in.

ABDOMINIS. *(beginning to be friendly to* **PATELLA-UTERUS,** *who is still very close to him)* You are correct as always, Pat.

PATELLA-UTERUS. Thank you…Abs. *(She giggles like a girl.)*

TOUCH. *(going over to* **LEONARDO***)* Well even if you are a bad mutant, it'd be bad like good-bad. Like gangsta. You know what I mean?

LEONARDO. I know what you mean, Touch. But I am change. A new thought. A new idea. A challenge to the rules. To the entrenched I am a threat. Good and bad are in the eye of the beholder. There are people who believe that killing your enemies is good. Some people think that belief in god is bad. Eating meat – mixed race children – good or bad? And the concept of good and bad changes with time. Long hair; dreadlocks – good or bad?

TIBIA. *(interjecting)* Oh, like CROCS *(or current fashion faux pas)* – baaaaaad.

LEONARDO. The same star that gives life to everything on earth will eventually destroy all of it. Is that good or bad? The concept of a universal good or a universal bad is very primitive.

TOUCH. I don't want to be primitive. I'm on Facebook *(or current technology)* for god's sake. Come on, Fruitcakes.

FEMORAL. I'm with you girlfriend.

*(***TOUCH*** *and* ***FEMORAL*** *move over to the side with* ***LEONARDO*** *and* ***SANDY***.*)*

(silence)

PONS. People, it has to be unanimous.

SANDY. *(puts down book, clears her throat)* Could I say something? If anyone remembers you were all let in here at one time or another. In the beginning, before intelligence, before aggression, before sex, there was just me, stringing little strands of amino acids together. Then Pons came along and he had some new and interesting ideas – some more organization. So I let him in. You all came bringing something new, and have proved your value. But if I hadn't of let anyone in, took no risk, the project would still be floating in a primordial soup on the tide. A few million years from now, we might be glad we let him in. He will solve problems, and bring problems to the project, but they will be new problems. And THAT is the only way we can progress.

*(***TIBIA*** *and* ***PATELLA-UTERUS*** *get up and go over to* ***LEONARDO***'s *side. Everyone stares at* ***HAMSTRING***, ***CEREBELLUM***, *and* ***ABDOMINIS*** *on the other side.)*

PONS. You know I hate to be pushy, but we have two hundredths of a second to agree…

HAMSTRING. Plenty of time. Count me in. I say we go for a Hail Mary Pass. *(He crosses over.)*

CEREBELLUM. *(talking himself into it)* This all scares me. It's worse than a poetry test. I like math – I don't know poetry. Well I like songs. That is poetry, I guess. Ya know: *(sings a few bars of the previous iconic 60's song[**])* – I like that. Oh, what the hell – count me in.

*(Everyone stares at **ABDOMINIS** alone on the other side.)*

ABDOMINIS. *(defensive)* What? No, I agree. Do I really have to get up?

*(**TOUCH** and **FEMORAL** link hands in front of **LEON-ARDO** and the others spread out and do the same until everyone's arms are linked in a chain.)*

PONS. Is everyone ready…? Split.

(BLACKOUT. MUSIC. SWIRLS.)

[**] See Music Use Note on Page 3.

CALLING ALL PLAYWRIGHTS!

DRAMATIC DEBUTS
Baker's Plays High School Playwriting Competition

Be a published playwright…
Bring us your **BEST**, **BOLDEST** and most **BRILLIANT** plays.

Please visit BakersPlays.com for more information on how to submit your play and win!

Be sure to check out
DRAMATIC DEBUTS VOLUME 1,
featuring:

Writer's Block by Samuel French - 1st Place
Mechant Enfant by Samuel Mayer - 2nd Place
The Metronome by Gabriel Neudstadt - 3rd Place
Unwanted Adventure by Brandon Johnson - Honorable Mention

BAKERSPLAYS.COM